MW00563209

The Book of Abraham

The
Book
of
Abraham

A Biblical Version of
The American Civil War

Selected and Arranged by Joseph DeStefano

Contents

A Gift

"Great are the myths . . . . I too delight in them,
Great are Adam and Eve . . . . I too look back and accept them;
Great the risen and fallen nations, and their poets, women, sages,
* inventors, rulers, warriors and priests.*
Great is liberty! Great is equality! I am their follower...

Great is today, and beautiful,
It is good to live in this age . . . . there never was any better.

Great are the plunges and throes and triumphs and falls of democracy...
Great are yourself and myself...

Great is the greatest nation . . . the nation of clusters of equal
* nations...."*

(Whitman, "Great Are the Myths")

The more entrenched we become in our own day of
hyper-polarity, the more astonishing Walt Whitman is to me.
When he published his first edition of *Leaves of Grass* in 1855,
the country was hurling itself toward civil war. And yet, for
him, "today" is great. And "beautiful." And the United States
of America is the "greatest nation," however unpredictable its
"democracy." How could he say as much then? What faith
marshaled the way? What model did he hope to provide?

In the "Preface" of that same work, Whitman announces his own ideal of self, a person who "has the most faith" because he "sees farthest"—who "learns the lesson" and then is able to place "himself where the future becomes the present." 165 years later, right now, in what still has legitimate claim as being the most advanced nation in history, Whitman's "future-present" feels somehow again as far away as ever, or even farther, and that fact alone could reasonably lead one to dismiss his "faith" as laughable. But there is another fact that keeps at least me from doing so, and that fact is that Whitman may just as well have been describing a very real person, a man whose personal challenges and dynamism and leadership helped save the nation and its democracy from its own shortsightedness: Abraham Lincoln.

"A Biblical Version of the American Civil War" was initially a self-stylized paper I wrote for my *Bible as Literature* class, first semester of sophomore year in 1994. Then, I was experimenting, constructing a new American God, and retelling a segment of American history in the mold of the *Book of Judges*—audacious, yes, but, as always, respectful (see the original "Note to My Professor" in the back of the book). Now, in 2020, stuck fast in a nation convulsing with monstrous, even terroristic xenophobia and proud paranoia, and hurling its heft recklessly at global environmental collapse; and after having read and learned much about the American Civil War, and about the various personalities connected to it, and about many things besides, not least of which is my own susceptibility to a narrowness of perspective, this old paper, this project, strikes me as especially relevant. Not merely experimental any more, I hope it is remedial.

But why this form—this vehicle? Is it not blasphemous? But that is exactly the opposite of my intention. When Homer brings gods to the battlefield to fight alongside mortals, he is stating emphatically: "This matters!" And that is part of what I am doing here as well. This, our heritage of words and many deeds, great and small, grandiose and petty—these sundry measures of devotion to an identity and an ideal—such spirit of action as characterizes the course of our whole history, and of our Civil War in particular—it all matters, too—matters cosmically. And certainly, the magnificent work and startling genius of those referenced and oft-quoted verbatim here are, I believe, worthy of all reverence—of the divine treatment, as they say. See for yourself—"See it with your eyes" (*Deuteronomy* 34.4). It is nothing new, only forgotten, waiting, as Whitman would say, under our bootsoles.

The point here is to make a gift of at least part of what we can call our common heritage, a gift of all these many works, and of the figures portrayed in them. In its new form, I hope this version of the American Civil War might both inform our current discourse, and change its tone. Mine is not, therefore, a historical endeavor at all. It is a spiritual one. I take up the spiritual content of our worst national crisis to date in an attempt to inspire us to ask and answer old questions anew— within ourselves. The book's greatest reward, I hope, will be, as much for you as it was for me, wholly personal—affecting each of the songs of ourselves.

Yes, *The Book of Abraham* is a gift to my children, and to my father and mother; and it is a gift to all children and fathers and mothers all over the world forever and ever. Emerson said of Lincoln: "I am sure if this man had ruled in a period of less facility of printing, he would have become mythological in a very few years." More than a few years have passed since Lincoln's "fables and proverbs" helped navigate our forebears through civil war, but perhaps, in this period of ubiquitous text-toxicity and bescreened somnambulism, his awe-inspiring genius can cut through in mythic proportions again, and help us. For we are both what we have been and what we can be, and still I hope and believe we can embrace Whitman's "future-present" in ourselves, and march ourselves more faithfully towards its beauty—towards its higher ideal.

To my children,

and to all myth-makers everywhere.

The
Book
of
Abraham

I

1 The Lord, the God of the United States of America, speaks: "To me the converging objects of the universe perpetually flow. Divine am I inside and out, and I make holy whatever I touch or am touched by."[1] And the People of the United States knew the Lord was right, and they knew she was good. They trusted in her always. The Lord speaks again: "You are the race of races, and here is not merely a nation, but a teeming nation of nations. To it the other continents arrive as contributions; and sure as the most certain sure, to it all nations of all continents will arrive one day—the smallest the same and the largest the same."[2] Learned and unlearned felt that it was so, and the People praised the Lord, their God.[3]

Then the Constitution was constructed in fire, the Constitution of the People, by the People, and for the People of the United States, but it was not perfect, and the People knew it. It was contradictory, in fact, on point of its highest ideal— seeded with God's greater glory, with her desire for all her children, for all men and women all over the world, but planted in ignorant and cruel compromise. "Mortal works are imperfect, but the People are dignified insofar as they reach, work, and suffer for perfection,"[4] the Lord says. She looked on the People's Constitution, and said, "No origin is like where it leads to."[5] And the nation of nations did prosper.

---

[1] Whitman, *Leaves of Grass* (1855), pp. 45, 51

[2] Whitman, *Leaves of Grass* (1855), pp. 7, 5, 28, 42

[3] Whitman, *Leaves of Grass* (1855), p. 28

[4] Shenk, *Lincoln's Melancholy*, p. 208

[5] Rumi, *The Essential Rumi*

2 But the Lord soon cursed the land. Some of the People said unto themselves, "Look, we are now one People, and we all have one language; and nothing we propose to do will now be impossible."[6] But they were not one together, and the Lord saw through their hypocrisy—she saw that their wickedness, their willful blindness, their regressive acquiescence and fear persisted, north and south, east and west, and it grieved her in her heart.[7] The Lord said unto herself, "If any of them without knowing it, are doing any of the things that by my guidance ought not to be done, they have incurred guilt and are subject to punishment.[8] And especially is slavery a scourge upon me!" The Lord, the God of the United States of America, saw the People dividing themselves, confused in their language and stuck in their ways, and she was sorry to see it.[9]

Many of the People knew slavery was evil, but many also did make believe it was not. They quoted the Lord, "To it, the nation of America, all the other People of all the other continents arrive as contributions: I am the Lord, your God." And they gazed at the Blacks because they were dark and made them keep the fields.[10] They said unto the Blacks, "You shall keep my statutes and my ordinances; by doing so you shall live."[11] And the Blacks answered in fear, "Everything the

[6] Genesis 11.6, *The New Oxford Annotated Bible*
[7] Genesis 6.5-6, *The New Oxford Annotated Bible*
[8] Leviticus 5.17, *The New Oxford Annotated Bible*
[9] Genesis 6.6, *The New Oxford Annotated Bible*
[10] Song of Solomon 1.6, *The New Oxford Annotated Bible*
[11] Leviticus 18.5, *The New Oxford Annotated Bible*

master has spoken we will do."[12] And even like so, they
became part of the People.

But the Lord speaks: "I am not an earth nor an adjunct of
an earth. I am the mate and companion of People, and all the
men ever born, any where, are also brothers, and the women
are sisters, and all are my lovers, and a kelson of the creation is
love."[13] And yet ill means seemed necessary in the thoughts
and the hearts of too many of the People—necessary for their
"God-ordained" prosperity and their good, they believed; and
so expedience and casuistry crowned their days, and too many
of the People huzzahed those who cited scripture for their own
purposes.[14] And in the South, in particular, talk of the abolition
of slavery was made to seem a clear and present danger to their
own freedom—to their very identity as part of the People. Talk
even of secession arose among them. Talk even of war.

Many Southerners, as well as Northerners, watched the
rapid sequence of events in horror but felt unable to do much
about it.[15] The best educated were the least inclined to take
threats seriously, dismissing them as too absurd to last.[16]
Sebastian Haffner in one of the papers of the People wrote:
"Everything takes place under a kind of anesthesia. Objectively
dreadful events produce a thin, puny emotional response.
Murders are committed like schoolboy pranks. Humiliation
and moral decay are accepted like minor incidents."[17] But
many of the People, consumed completely with themselves,

[12] Exodus 19.8, *The New Oxford Annotated Bible*

[13] Whitman, *Leaves of Grass* (1855), pp. 33, 31

[14] Shakespeare, *The Merchant of Venice*, I. iii. 90 (p. 219)

[15] Bakewell, *At the Existenstialist Café*, p. 75

[16] Bakewell, *At the Existenstialist Café*, p. 76

[17] Haffner, quoted in *At the Existenstialist Café*, p.77

and with each of their various kinds, were unafraid, and were stuck fast in the echo chambers of mendacity. In the South, they called for secession—for a still newer, truer nation, and they said, "The Lord shall deliver us from oppression just as she did before, and she will defend us again and ever again until each man and woman and dog constitutes his or her own nation, independent, free, and fearful!" And so they argued, and defended slavery as necessary for their prosperity and their present good.

3 The People were corrupt in God's sight, and the United States of America was replete with the degenerative malignancy of the now brimming, now singling resort to violence.[18] Preston Brooks of South Carolina attacked Charles Sumner of Massachusetts with a tent peg and a mallet on the floor of the United States Senate—attacked Sumner and left him for dead. "So perish all your enemies, O Lord!" Brooks called out, "and may your friends be like the sun as it rises in its might."[19] God saw that the People and the land were corrupt, and she saw that nothing should now hold back their punishment—hold back the floods of war.[20]

Then Abraham Lincoln rose to power in the North. Lamech of Uz in the west said,

> *"Out of the ground that the Lord has cursed,*

---

[18] Genesis 6.11, *The New Oxford Annotated Bible*

[19] Judges 5.31, *The New Oxford Annotated Bible*

[20] Genesis 6.17, *The New Oxford Annotated Bible*

this one shall bring us relief.[21]
Out of loose ends insufficiency,
    'The Rail Splitter' now emerges,
from father unfit, and late mother down—
        late mother, late sister, and son,
        the milk sick, stillborn, his very own
        down, down and done,
done.
From tomorrow, tomorrow, and tomorrow,[22]
from failure upon failure, and frontier—
        from the western edge of this still emerging,
        still wanting, still burgeoning, broken,
        dying nation, Abraham steps into the clear.
And from the fatal first of Jany '41,
        from '54 and '55, '57, and very now,
        sleepless, ambitious, unschooled, and sad,
        but resilient, ever wise and good,
        this one, I tell you, shall bring us relief,
        this one shall restore our hopes."

Lamech Oglesby of Uz then concluded:

"Man, too, is born broken.
    Abraham lives by mending.
        The grace of God is his glue."[23]

And God saw the stalwart and wellshaped heir who approached.[24] She walked with him, and said, "Abraham, the

---

[21] Genesis 5.29, *The New Oxford Annotated Bible*
[22] Shakespeare, *Macbeth*, V. v. 19 (p. 1133)
[23] O'Neill, quoted in *Lincoln's Melancholy*, p. 193

nation is filled with hatred and violence, and the People together with animals and creeping things and birds of the air are in danger; all flesh in which is the breath of life, and everything else that is on the earth, or that may ever be, has its stake in this crisis.[25] But I will establish my covenant with you.[26] Make an ark of the Union, and a creed of those words 'all are created equal,' and remember how imperfect perfection appears.[27] None will see my truth clearly, not even those who should know me best, not even you; but believe, Abraham, that what is true for you in your private heart is true for all People.[28] I will be there and will teach you what you are to speak.[29] Then shall they know I am the Lord their God, who brought from them the better angels of their nature so that I might dwell among them."[30]

4 But the People were confused and angry, skeptical to the last of Lincoln, believing too well the bias of their living, breathing eyes and ears. Secession of the States of the South already seemed certain, and questions arose all over, and prophesies and prognostications, all highly regarded, spread. "You ask me if I think your visions are true," Abraham Lincoln began to respond in writing: "they are true if they make you

---

[24] Whitman, *Leaves of Grass* (1855), p. 5

[25] Genesis 6.7, and 6.17, *The New Oxford Annotated Bible*

[26] Genesis 6.18, *The New Oxford Annotated Bible*

[27] Genesis 6.14, *The New Oxford Annotated Bible*

[28] Emerson, "Self Reliance", p. 147

[29] Exodus 4.12, *The New Oxford Annotated Bible*

[30] Exodus 29.46, *The New Oxford Annotated Bible*

become more human, more kind to every creature and plant that you know."[31]

"But we are conservatives," one of the People from the South responded, "and we favor democracy, we do, and we are willing to support whichever way the vote may go."[32]

"Conservative?" Abraham wrote. "All decent slave-holders and peaceful gun-owners talk that way. But they never vote that way. Our progress in degeneracy appears to me to be pretty rapid. As a nation, we began by declaring that 'all are created equal.' We now practically read it, 'all are created equal, except negroes.' If the Know-Nothings get control, it will read, 'all are created equal, except negroes, and foreigners, and catholics, and women.' And if the so called American Party should trump us now, I should prefer emigrating to some other country where they make no pretense of loving liberty— to Russia, for instance, where despotism can be taken pure, and without the base alloy of hypocracy."[33]

And in the North, mere chaos ensued. Stephen A. Douglas, the Little Giant, also of the west, and a successful politician, a democrat, who played for all the chances, and like a skillful gambler never let the logic of principle displace the logic of success, opposed Lincoln's every syllable.[34] Edward Everett, whose scholarly reputation thrust him into a position of trust, a role he relished, even as such relish led too easily, too quickly to his own proud sense of certainty, concluded: "Lincoln is evidently a person of very inferior cast of character,

[31] Hafiz, *The Gift*

[32] Shenk, *Lincoln's Melancholy*, p. 145

[33] Lincoln, quoted in *Lincoln's Melancholy*, pp. 145, 6

[34] Lincoln, quoted in *Lincoln's Melancholy*, p. 150

wholly unequal to the crisis we are now in."[35]   Frederick
Douglass, the slave who would not hide in the shadow, the
Runaway who runs towards struggle—towards its crowning
truth—even he, Frederick Douglass, refused to support him,
knowing Lincoln's suspect record on Black rights.[36] Indeed, all
the radicals of Lincoln's own party were dissatisfied almost to
the point of disgust with this equivocating nominee from the
western frontier. The eyes of princes, nobles, aristocrats, of
dukes, earls, scholars, statesmen, warriors, all turned on the
plain backwoodsman, watched him with a fearful curiosity, and
simply asked, "Will that awkward old backwoodsman really get
that ship through?"[37]

But the Lord, the God of the United States of America,
walked with Abraham, and she said unto herself, "He shall be
fittest for his days."[38]

 In the eighty-fourth year of the new republic, in
the second month, on the twenty-seventh day of
the month, Abraham Lincoln stepped up to the
podium in the Great Hall to speak to the
People.[39] He wore a new suit that did not fit

[35] Everett, quoted in *Lincoln's Melancholy*, p. 172

[36] Kendi, *Stamped from the Beginning*, p. 212

[37] Harriet Beecher Stowe, quoted in *Lincoln's Melancholy*, p. 172

[38] Whitman, *Leaves of Grass* (1855), p. 5

[39] Shenk, *Lincoln's Melancholy*, p. 163

well, and appeared ungainly, unbecoming before their eyes, his own eyes ghostly pale, and he spoke in a high-pitched, breathy voice: "A house divided against itself cannot stand."[40]

"Old fellow," many of the People in the Great Hall thought, "You will not do."[41]

But Lincoln proceeded:

"Slave-holders, slave-traders, secessionists,
*   your maxims are proverbs of ashes.[42]*
You say you are conservative—
*   eminently conservative,*
*   but what is conservatism?*

I stick to, contend for, the identical old policy
*   on the point in controversy*
which was adopted by 'our fathers
*   who framed the Government*
*   under which we live';*
while you with one accord reject,
*   and scout, and spit upon that old policy,*
*   and insist upon substituting something new.[43]*

Would not your brand of conservatism
*   make, unmake, do as you list,*
*   even as your appetites play the god*
*   with our weak function?[44]*

---

[40] Lincoln, *The Portable Abraham Lincoln*, p. 89
[41] Shenk, *Lincoln's Melancholy*, p. 162
[42] Job 13.12, *The New Oxford Annotated Bible*
[43] Lincoln, quoted in *Lincoln's Melancholy*, p. 163

Would we not then arm ourselves
    against ourselves infinitely,
and call our murderous paranoia pride of identity?

And would we not build walls
    and call our fellow human beings
    monsters and criminals,
and expect no third party to intervene,
    nor object?[45]

Would we not serve our present so blindly,
    so absolutely, as to poison the very earth
    of our future—
    legally and with holier-than-thou obstinacy?"

The People in the Great Hall found themselves in silent awe, and the People of the United States of America, and all the People all over the world did too, each one leaning in to hear Lincoln's stentorian subtlety. In the expectant pause, Abraham thought to himself, "If it is decreed that I should go down because of this speech, then let me go down linked to the truth."[46]   He surged again from his heart, though starting slowly:

"No, friends, let us not stand by
    and look on merely.

---

[44] Shakespeare, *Othello*, II. iii. 329-31 (p. 1035)

[45] Lincoln, quoted in *Lincoln's Melancholy*, p. 150

[46] Lincoln, quoted in *Lincoln's Melancholy*, p. 151

*Let us, rather, stand by our duty
  fearlessly and effectively.*

*Let us not be diverted by none of these
    sophistical contrivances,
wherewith we are so industriously plied and belabored—
    contrivances such as groping for some middle ground
    between the right and the wrong:
        vain as the search for a man who should be
        neither a living man nor a dead man;
such as a policy of 'don't care' on a question
    about which all true People do care;
such as Union appeals beseeching true Unionists
    to yield to Disunionists, reversing the divine rule,
    and calling, not the sinners, but the righteous,
    to repentance.[47]*

*No, nor let our silence speak falsely for God—
    speak deceitfully for her, for our one mother, too.[48]*

*LET US HAVE FAITH, RATHER,
    THAT RIGHT MAKES MIGHT,
AND IN THAT FAITH LET US TO THE END
    DARE TO DO OUR DUTY
        AS WE UNDERSTAND IT."[49]*

And the People began to applaud uproariously, but
Abraham Lincoln lifted his hand to hold them off a moment

---

[47] Lincoln, *The Portable Abraham Lincoln*, p. 186
[48] Job 13.7, *The New Oxford Annotated Bible*
[49] Lincoln, *The Portable Abraham Lincoln*, p. 187

longer, his eyes seemed now to blaze forth with otherworldly power. The Great Hall grew silent again, and Abraham continued:

> *"Our republican robe is soiled,*
> *and trailed in the dust.*
> *Let us purify it.*
> *Let us turn and wash it in the spirit,*
> *if not the blood, of the Revolution.*
> *And let all the People, North and South—*
> *let all lovers of liberty everywhere*
> *join in the great and good work."*[50]

The crowd could hardly restrain itself, but Abraham spoke louder: "If we do this..." Silence masked a great upsurge in all the People's hearts. . . .

> *"If we do this,*
> *we shall not only have saved the Union;*
> *but we shall have so saved it as to make, and keep it,*
> *forever worthy of the saving."*

Then louder still he said:

> *"We shall have so saved it,*
> *that the succeeding millions*
> *of free happy People,*
> *the world over,*
> *shall rise up, and call us blessed,*
> *to the latest generations."*[51]

---

[50] Lincoln, quoted in *Lincoln's Melancholy*, p. 147
[51] Lincoln, quoted in *Lincoln's Melancholy*, p. 147

Abraham fell off, and, at last, the mass exploded before him—they whooped, and whistled, and stamped their feet.[52] But he stepped from the podium in the Great Hall diffident, and sad.[53] The great and good work before him seemed never so daunting as it did through the prism of his success. How confused, how conflicted he knew he still was about everything he put forth.

But the Lord smiled unto herself again, and said, "Yes, he shall be fittest."[54]

 Abraham Lincoln was elected President of the United States, but many of the People still doubted his mettle, or outright rejected his new authority, especially the representatives of the People in the South.

In closed-door sessions, Abraham said to his newly chosen ministers, "We must settle this question now, whether in a free government the minority have the right to break up the government whenever they choose."[55]

And at his inaugural address, beneath the half-completed and roofless Capitol Building, he spoke directly to the People of the South:

[52] Shenk, *Lincoln's Melancholy*, p. 163

[53] Shenk, *Lincoln's Melacholy*, p. 164

[54] Whitman, *Leaves of Grass* (1855), p. 5

[55] Lincoln, quoted in *Lincoln's Melancholy*, p. 171

"In your hands,
*   my dissatisfied fellow countrymen,*
*   and not in mine,*
is the momentous issue of civil war.

You have no oath registered in Heaven
*   to destroy the government of the People,*
while I shall have the most solemn one
*   to 'preserve, protect, and defend' it.*

We are not enemies, but friends.
*   We must not be enemies.*
Though passion may have strained,
*   it must not break our bonds of affection.*
The mystic chords of memory,
*   stretching from every battlefield,*
*   and patriot grave,*
*   to every living hearthstone,*
*   all over this broad land,*
will yet swell the chorus of the Union,
*   when again touched, as surely they will be,*
*   by the better angels of our nature."*[56]

The South seceded the next day, as the Lord knew they would. And the armies of the North and the South prepared for war against each other. Brother and brother divided, and sister, and mother, father and son, friends, and one-time allies, all, all things under the sun were inundated by the sense of the inevitable war. A tenuous line was drawn between the People, between very families, North and South, Unionist, or Federal,

---

[56] Lincoln, *The Portable Abraham Lincoln*, p. 204

Confederate, or Rebel, Invader, Instigator, Confused, the Gray, and the Blue, and both sides, and all sides were under the Lord.

> *"I am of old and young,*
> > *of the foolish as much as the wise,*
> *Paternal as well as Maternal,*
> > *of the woman the same as the man,"*[57]

The Lord, the God of the United States of America declaims,

> *"A Southerner soon as a Northerner,*
> > *a planter nonchalant and hospitable,*
> *A Yankee bound my own way,*
> *A Kentuckian walking the vale of the Elkhorn,*
> *A boatman over the lakes or bays or along coasts,*
> > *a Hoosier, a Badger, a Buckeye,*
> *A Louisianian or Georgian,*
> > *a poke-easy from the sandhills and pines,*
> *At home on the hills of Vermont,*
> *At home in the woods of Maine,*
> *At home on a Texan ranch,*
> *Comrade of Californians,*
> > *and of free northwesterners,*
> > > *of all who shake hands and welcome*
> > > > *to drink and meat,*
> *For the illiterate, and for the judges of the Supreme Court,*
> *For the Federal capitol and the State capitols,*
> *For the endless races of working People*
> > *and farmers and seamen—*
> *I am of every hue and trade and rank,*

---

[57] Whitman, *Leaves of Grass* (1855), pp. 42

of every caste and religion,
Not merely of the New World but of Africa Europe or Asia—
I will not have a single person slighted or left away.[58]

Yes, through me many long dumb voices,
Voices of the interminable generations of slaves,
Voices of prostitutes and of deformed persons,
Voices of the diseased and despairing,
Voices of the cycles of preparation and accretion,
*   and of the threads that connect the stars—*
*   and of wombs,*
*   and of the fatherstuff,*
And of the rights of them the others are down upon,
Of the trivial and flat and foolish and despised—[59]
There shall be no difference between them and the rest,[60]
*   for whoever degrades another degrades me,*
*   and whatever is done or said returns at last to me,*
*   and whatever I do or say I also return."*[61]

And the Lord sings out:

"We have had ducking and deprecating about enough.
I chant a new chant of dilation or pride,[62]
*   In all the People I see myself,*
*   none more and not one a barleycorn less."*[63]

---

[58] Whitman, *Leaves of Grass* (1855), p. 42-4

[59] Whitman, *Leaves of Grass* (1855), p. 50

[60] Whitman, *Leaves of Grass* (1855), p. 44

[61] Whitman, *Leaves of Grass* (1855), p. 50

[62] Whitman, *Leaves of Grass* (1855), p. 47

[63] Whitman, *Leaves of Grass* (1855), p. 45

7 Then Jefferson Davis rose to power in the South, and all the People wondered, "Is Jefferson Davis also among the prophets?[64] Where is he from?" they asked.

And he answered, "From going to and fro on the earth, and from walking up and down on it."[65]

And once in power, he first sought to clean house. He ordered the capitulation of Fort Sumter in Charleston, South Carolina, which was occupied and guarded by a small Union troop. With caution in every letter, Abraham Lincoln ordered the Navy of the North to bring the besieged garrison provisions, but with no arms, and without any additional soldiers. Neither he, nor Jeff Davis wanted to fire the first shot. Major General Robert Anderson, a Kentuckian married to a Georgian, defended the fort for the Blue, among whom he still proudly numbered himself. But his own former student at West Point, a Louisianan Creole, General P.G.T. Beauregard, now trained Southern canon on the U.S. installation.[66]

Then the Navy of the North sailed forth.

And then Jefferson Davis ordered P.G.T. Beauregard to reduce the fort. P.G.T. Beauregard then told Roger Pryor, the Virginian fire-eater, to strike a blow! Roger Pryor asked Edmund Ruffin, a white-haired, old-line secessionist, sixty-seven years of age, and also from Virginia, to fire the first shot,[67] and Edmund Ruffin said, "They shall tear down our

---

[64] 1 Samuel 10.11, *The New Oxford Annotated Bible*

[65] Job 1.7, *The New Oxford Annotated Bible*

[66] Foote, *The Civil War*, v. 1, p. 48

[67] Foote, *The Civil War*, v. 1, p. 51

alters, break our pillars, and cut down our sacred poles. And they, and the Blacks, yes, even the Blacks, shall take wives from among our daughters."[68] In South Carolina, the People had heard such talk from their preachers, from their church bodies, from their periodicals, from their politicians for years—there especially, the only state in the union with a Black majority.[69] Most fiercely, and most fearfully, Edmund Ruffin fired the first shot.

[68] Exodus 34.13, and 34.16, *The New Oxford Annotated Bible*
[69] Kendi, *Stamped from the Beginning*, p. 213

II

8 After the capitulation of Sumter, the People in the North asked Abraham Lincoln, "Who shall go down first to fight against the Rebels?"

Abraham replied, "Irvin McDowell, the Ohioan, shall go down."[70]

And so, on July 21, 1861, Irvin McDowell led fifty regiments of infantry, ten batteries of field artillery, and one battalion of cavalry, the largest and finest army on the continent, into Virginia, toward Richmond, the new capital of the South, where Jefferson Davis took up his office.[71] P.G.T. Beauregard, earlier summoned from South Carolina, rushed with little more than half as many soldiers, to take defensive position against McDowell, north of the railway junction Manassas, where the Bull Run river flows.

But in the ranks of the army of the South there was a soldier, the youngest of the eight sons of Jesse, a fire-eater of Virginia, and a general, who said to his superiors, "Let no one's heart fail because of this enemy."[72] His name was Thomas Jonathan Jackson, and to those in his charge he said, "What is life without honor? Degradation is worse than death."[73] His soldiers believed the Lord was with him, and they trusted him completely, while those ranked above him could not make out his value.

When the army of the North drew nearer to meet the army of the South at Manassas, Thomas Jonathan Jackson refused to

---

[70] Judges 1.1-2, *The New Oxford Annotated Bible*

[71] Foote, *The Civil War*, v. 1, p. 70, 1

[72] 1 Samuel 17.32, *The New Oxford Annotated Bible*

[73] Jackson, quoted in *The Civil War*, v. 1, p. 65

back away despite being heavily outnumbered.[74] The rest of
the army of the South was giving ground, but Jackson stood
strong.

One of his reeling superiors cried out, "Look! There is
Jackson standing like a stone wall! Let us determine to die
here, and we will conquer."[75]

Jackson, himself, told his charge calmly, despite being
pressed by yet another wave of Bluecoats, "Hold your fire until
they're on you. Then fire and give them the bayonet." His
soldiers listened to him, and dismissed their fear. "And, when
you charge," Jackson added, "yell like the furies!"[76]

And when they did as he had commanded them, the
tide of the battle changed completely: the army of the South
rallied around them, and the shocked Union troops were
routed: the Bluecoats skedaddled all the way back to
Washington—back to where they started. And henceforth
Thomas Jonathan Jackson was called Stonewall, and no person
of rank, above or below, ever again doubted his value.

That evening, after all reports were confirmed, Abraham
Lincoln asked the Lord, "Why? Why have you dealt the North
a defeat? Why have you dealt the United States a blow?"

And the Lord answered, "I say it is good to fall. Battles are
lost in the same spirit in which they are won."[77]

---

[74] 1 Samuel 17.48, *The New Oxford Annotated Bible*

[75] Foote, *The Civil War*, v. 1, p. 78

[76] Jackson, quoted in *The Civil War*, v. 1, p. 80

[77] Whitman, *Leaves of Grass* (1855), p. 44

Abraham was not comforted by this. He stood in silence at his office window, and after a pause, wondered aloud, "Why have you made me your target? Why have I become a burden to you?"[78] Rain fell outside, and wave upon wave of defeated soldier straggled past his window.

Lincoln then closed his eyes, swallowed deeply, and submitted aloud, "Blessed be the name of the Lord."[79]

Then the Lord, the God of the United States of America, responded, "I will never break my covenant with you.[80] This is what you shall do: Create two armies and appoint Ulysses S. Grant the general of one, and George B. McClellan the general of the other. The former will bring you victories, the latter will give Washington its place of stand, and its pride." And Abraham did as the Lord knew he would.

9 Ulysses S. Grant, in the west, took Fort Henry and Fort Donelson in short order, wresting with each a badly needed river from the South, and some badly needed confidence for the North. Then Ulysses marched his army into Tennessee, the Confederates, and the Confederacy, seeming to evaporate before his every step. Nashville, the first State capital conceded by the Secessionists, went without a fight, and Jefferson Davis, in his over-sized office in Richmond felt humiliated.

But then he turned to his favorite, a champion named Albert Sydney Johnston, whose height was six cubits and a

---

[78] Job 7.20, *The New Oxford Annotated Bible*
[79] Job 1.21, *The New Oxford Annotated Bible*
[80] Judges 2.1, *The New Oxford Annotated Bible*

span.[81]   To this general, Jefferson Davis also sent P.G.T. Beauregard once again—sent him, superstitious of his luck.

Ulysses S. Grant struck camp before the southern border of Tennessee, near a log church named Shiloh—Shiloh, "the place of peace."[82]   And there, right behind that church, on a simple bed, in the evening light of April 5, 1862, William Tecumseh Sherman reflected on the war. He was another West Pointer, and also like Grant, an Ohioan, who, prior to the war between the States, was the superintendent of the Louisiana State Military Academy; but, more than all of these, he was now Grant's most trusted general.[83]   To him, and to his green division, the largest of the army, Ulysses S. Grant awarded the position of honor, farthest in the front, just before the church called Shiloh, where Sherman rested, waiting for the morning push west into Mississippi.[84]

But opposite William Tecumseh Sherman, preparing in the dark, Davis's champion Albert Sydney Johnston, Johnston the Great, planned to launch a bold and redemptive strike in the morning. "Tomorrow," he said, "I defy the ranks of the North!"[85]   Behind Johnston was Beauregard, and behind Beauregard was Breckinridge, and behind Breckinridge was a soldier, a cavalry officer, a Memphis slave dealer, and Mississippi planter, who never read a book on war—who had had little formal schooling of any kind, in fact, but who had shown an uncanny aptitude for war.[86] His name was Nathan

---

[81] 1 Samuel 17.4, *The New Oxford Annotated Bible*

[82] Foote, *The Civil War*, v. 1, p. 342

[83] Foote, *The Civil War*, v. 1, p. 58

[84] Foote, *The Civil War*, v. 1, p. 331

[85] 1 Samuel 17.10, *The New Oxford Annotated Bible*

[86] Foote, *The Civil War*, v. 1, p. 172

Bedford Forrest, and he was nothing if not critical.[87] He told his men, "War means fighting. And fighting means killing."[88] And even before the war he could kill most ruthlessly. Narrowly escaping Grant's capture of Fort Donelson, he now desired greater reckoning, and his soldiers were more than willing to help him to it.

10

When primal dawn spread on the eastern sky her fingers of pink light, Johnston the Great, sprang his attack.[89] The Bluecoats fell back, and William Tecumseh Sherman was shot, grazed once on the shoulder, and once through his hand; but still he stood, leaning against a tree, issuing orders. Position after rearward position his soldiers took, offering stiff resistance each time until again overwhelmed. Ulysses S. Grant then came himself to take full command, trying to stave off complete disaster.

Opposite him, riding front and center now, Albert Sydney Johnston stood in his stirrups, removed his hat, and called back to the ranks of Graycoats behind him, "I will lead you!"[90] And even like so, did the favorite of Jefferson Davis meet his end: a bullet sank into his leg, and severed his femoral artery.[91] He fell face down on the ground.[92]

----

[87] Shakespeare, *Othello*, II. i. 119 (p. 1030)

[88] Forrest, quoted in *The Civil War*, v. 1, p. 349

[89] Homer, *The Odyssey*, p. 19

[90] Foote, *The Civil War*, v. 1, p. 339

[91] Foote, *The Civil War*, v. 1, p. 339

[92] 1 Samuel 17.49, *The New Oxford Annotated Bible*

Still, his men carried on, leading themselves as they had been led.

One mile, two, the army of the North retreated in near desperation until it was, when fighting finally broke off, wedged between Snake Creek and the Tennessee River, ripe for annihilation, come morning. P.G.T. Beauregard, now in complete command of the army of the South in the west, rested with supreme gratification in the same makeshift bed Sherman had abandoned, and he wired Richmond, announcing that despite the grievous loss of Johnston, the South had scored a complete victory over Grant. What work remained for Beauregard and his soldiers to do appeared to him merely clerical.

Jefferson Davis learned this news, and murmured to himself, "Skin for skin, Abraham!"[93] But he was in great pain, himself. His left eye was diseased, and was beginning to bulge now, grotesquely enough that the orderly who brought him the telegram from Beauregard could not refrain from asking about it. Davis simply replied, "I only need one eye for an enemy such as this."

Back in Tennessee, rain fell in torrents that night on the two armies, and on the wounded, the dying, and the dead. Ulysses S. Grant could find no rest. William Tecumseh Sherman found him under a tree, chewing his cigar. Sherman said to him, "We've had the devil's own day, haven't we?" Grant concurred, but then added with a quick shift of the soggy cigar in his mouth, "Lick 'em tomorrow, though."[94]

---

[93] Job 2.4, *The New Oxford Annotated Bible*
[94] Grant and Sherman, quoted in *The Road to Shiloh*, p. 148

11 Dawn in her yellow robe rose in the east again,[95] and Ulysses S. Grant rose, too, commanding his army, amply reinforced throughout the night, "Advance and recapture our camps."[96] And, so they did. The army of the South, though much surprised by the reversal of their fortunes, gave ground no less stubbornly than did the army of the North the day before, but before the end of April 7, 1862, Grant's army had recovered all ground it had lost, and more. And P.G.T. Beauregard's army left the field entirely, but did so as though by choice, and started back to Corinth in Mississippi in the west.

Sherman gave pursuit with what little strength his weary army could muster, but Nathan Bedford Forrest of General Breckinridge's rearmost division halted it absolutely. Yes, Forrest, the cavalry colonel of Mississippi and of Tennessee, who never read a book on war, presently started rewriting it with a countercharge into the Union skirmishers.[97] Through them he and his charge rode, and through the opposing cavalry as well, until, siphoning off his companions, Forrest found himself alone, confronted with a wall of blue, an entire brigade of Sherman's infantry, shocked but unmoving.

One Union officer stepped to him, at last, and shot him with a pistol pressed against his side, the force lifting him up out of his saddle for an instant.[98] But Nathan Bedford Forrest sawed his horse around, grabbed another unsuspecting Federal by the collar, swung him onto the crupper of his horse, and

---

[95] Homer, *The Iliad*, p. 457

[96] Grant, quoted in *The Civil War*, v. 1, p. 346

[97] Foote, *The Civil War*, v. 1, p. 349

[98] Foote, *The Civil War*, v. 1, p. 350

galloped back to safety, using the hapless fellow as a shield against the bullets fired after him.[99]   No one on the field, neither in Gray nor Blue, was less than astonished by what Forrest had just done.   But the ball now lodged alongside his spine only spurred him the more, determined to be made by the war, or fordone quite by it.[100]   Sherman called off his pursuit, convinced the army of the South would linger no longer, and equally convinced his own soldiers could do nothing more to make sure of it.

The battle had been the most ghastly bloodbath in the history of the Western Hemisphere up to that time, America's baptism in total war, and both armies were utterly fought-out.[101] When evening came, Sherman reflected on the last two days of bloodletting, of fighting, shock, screaming and terror, and, resting again in the same simple bed of two nights before—the bed in a tent behind a church called Shiloh—"the place of peace," he shook his head, and sighed, "War is hell."[102]

12 In the east, another Johnston, General Joseph Egglesworth Johnston, scored an actual victory against George B. McClellan, but was wounded in the affair, and indefinitely incapacitated.   Jefferson Davis was happy enough to throw another defeat at the Invaders.   "Know then that God exacts of you less than your guilt deserves."[103] He was

---

[99] Foote, *The Civil War*, v. 1, p. 350

[100] Shakespeare, *Othello*, V. i. 129 (p. 1053)

[101] McPherson, *Ordeal by Fire*, p. 229

[102] Sherman, quoted in *Ordeal by Fire*, p. 461

[103] Job 11.6, *The New Oxford Annotated Bible*

thinking, as always, of Lincoln. Each word echoed back at him where he sat alone in his large Richmond office. But the loss of Johnston the Lesser on top of Johnston the Great gave him pause. If McClellan proved nothing else, he proved how resilient the North was. He could not just rally, but could replenish his army, and still he remained like a spiked collar around Richmond's neck.

"What shall I do?" Jefferson Davis asked. "Johnston upon Johnston? And with Albert Sydney," he admitted to himself, "our strongest pillar has been broken.[104] What shall I do?"

And the Lord, the God of America answered, "Very well,[105] you shall appoint Robert E. Lee general of the army of the South in the east. Who recruits him recruits horse and foot; he fetches parks of artillery the best that engineer ever knew. If the time becomes slothful and heavy, he knows how to arouse it. He can make every word he speaks draw blood."[106]

And Jefferson Davis did as the Lord knew he would.

For Lincoln, in Washington, the flood-waters of the war drew nigh. Indeed, Abraham was not sure he was not already drowning. George B. McClellan seemed utterly unwilling to use the army he rallied and rebuilt. Many misgivings accompanied the appointment of McClellan to command, the chief cause of which were his political leanings. He was a Democrat, strongly against the

[104] Davis, quoted in *The Civil War*, v. 1, p. 351
[105] Job 2.6, *The New Oxford Annotated Bible*
[106] Whitman, *Leaves of Grass* (1855), pg. 9

abolition of slavery, and though he had voted only once before the war, that vote was for none other than Stephen A. Douglas, Lincoln's greatest political rival. McClellan was an excellent organizer, and the army responded enthusiastically to him,[107] but now, through a series of excuses and miscalculations, over the course of almost an entire year, he had refused to give the enemy any battle. He brought his vastly superior numbers to settle close to Richmond, but, in truth, it was a retreat from Washington as much as from the battlefield: a show of force, but only a show. Little Mac, his men called him, a diminutive name, Lincoln thought, for a diminutive hope.

Sensing his opponent's hesitancy, the newly appointed commanding general Robert E. Lee, now heading the army he renamed the Army of Northern Virginia, lashed out at the army of the North. In seven days and seven nights, he sent it crawling back to Washington, back to where it started.

With McClellan's retrograde movement in the east, and with Grant's army stalled in the west, pressure mounted around Abraham from every quarter and critic, from every faction of his own government, and from the People themselves in the North. "Let us alone," everyone seemed to say.[108] Walt Whitman, the good gray poet, among the People, remarked to himself, "No one can really comprehend Lincoln's position, unless he understands the great fund of slavery feeling here in the North as well as in the South. Indeed, Northern sympathy is the hardest to bear, posing the knottiest problems."[109] Talk

---

[107] McPherson, *Ordeal by Fire*, pp. 213-5
[108] Exodus 14.12, *The New Oxford Annotated Bible*
[109] Whitman, quoted in *Walt Whitman Speaks*, p. 132

of foreign intervention on behalf of the South was heard, which, of course, would scuttle everything.

But the chief cause of aggravation as much as of the malaise of the People, Lincoln believed, was Little Mac's curious inaction. Frederick Douglass, the abolitionist orator, and tribune of the People,[110] said, "I feel quite sure that this country will yet come to the conclusion that George B. McClellan is either a cold blooded Traitor, or that he is an unmitigated military Imposter."[111]

It had already been rumored that McClellan's true intention was to hold out until he could run for president, himself, against Lincoln in '64, win, and then sue for peace with the South. Imagine the Union being reconstructed on the old and corrupting basis of compromise, by which slavery would retain all the power it ever had, with the full assurance of gaining more, according to its future necessities.[112] For Frederick Douglass, this prospect seemed all but certain. He said:

> *"Any attempt now to separate*
> *the freedom of the slave*
> *from the victory of our Government,*
> *any attempt to secure peace to the Whites*
> *while leaving the Blacks in chains*
> *will be labor lost.*
>
> *The American People*
> *may refuse to recognize it for a time;*
> *but the 'inexorable logic of events'*

---

[110] McPherson, *The Negro's Civil War*, p. 7
[111] Douglass, quoted in *The Negro's Civil War*, p. 46
[112] McPherson, *The Negro's Civil War*, p. 47

will force it upon them in the end
that the war now being waged in this land
is a war for and against slavery;
and that it can never be effectually put down
till one or the other of these vital forces
is completely destroyed.[113]

And how can one effectually suppress
and put down this desolating war
which the slaveholders and their Rebel minions
are now waging against the Government
and its loyal citizens?

Fire must be met with water,
darkness with light,
and war for the destruction of liberty
must be met with war for the destruction of slavery.

Freedom to the slave should now, therefore, be proclaimed
from the Capitol, and should be seen
above the smoke and fire of every battlefield,
waving from every loyal flag.[114]
Arrest the hoe in the hands of the negro,
and you smite rebellion
in the very seat of its life."[115]

Then replicating Lincoln's own style, he sang:

---

[113] Douglass, quoted in *The Negro's Civil War*, p. 17
[114] Douglass, quoted in *The Negro's Civil War*, pp. 37, 8
[115] Douglass, quoted in *The Negro's Civil War*, p. 39

"*Could we write as with lightning,*
and speak as with the voice of thunder,
we should write and cry to the nation:
REPENT, BREAK EVERY YOKE,
LET THE OPPRESSED GO FREE.
FOR HEREIN ALONE
IS DELIVERANCE AND SAFETY![116]

---

[116] Douglass, quoted in *The Negro's Civil War*, p. 17

III

14

Abraham Lincoln met with General George B. McClellan, and explained, "These are not the days of miracles. I must study the plain physical facts of the case, ascertain what is possible and learn what appears to be wise and right."[117] Little Mac sat uncomprehendingly before his president. "You're fired," Lincoln said. He then replaced McClellan with John Pope, and within a month, General John Pope took the army of the North in the east and charged headlong again at Manassas Junction in Virginia, where Robert E. Lee and Stonewall Jackson were waiting for him.

On August 30, 1862, a messenger came to Abraham Lincoln, and said: "Sir, General Pope has been kicked, cuffed, hustled about, knocked down, run over, and trodden upon as rarely happens in the history of war.[118] I alone from my regiment have escaped to tell you."[119] And the rest of the army of the North came crawling back to Washington, back to where it started. Abraham went into his quarters, alone. "If I am righteous, I cannot lift up my head, for I am filled with disgrace," he said. "O Lord, you renew your witness against me, and increase your vexation toward me; you bring fresh troops against me.[120] You make nations great, then destroy them. You strip understanding from me, and make me grope in the dark without light. You make me stagger like a drunkard."[121]

---

[117] Lincoln, quoted in *Lincoln's Melancholy*, p. 198

[118] Foote, *The Civil War*, v. 2, p. 642

[119] Job 1.15, *The New Oxford Annotated Bible*

[120] Job 10.17, *The New Oxford Annotated Bible*

[121] Job 12.23-25, *The New Oxford Annotated Bible*

A knock then came to his door. Abraham Lincoln looked at the door in silence. Then he whispered to himself, "The Lord gave, and the Lord has taken away; blessed be the name of the Lord."[122]

A second more urgent knock at the door, and Abraham answered. He was confronted by all his ministers. "What shall we do, Mr. President?" they cried.

After a pause, Abraham Lincoln said, "We must use the tools we have. There is no man in the army who can man these fortifications and lick these troops of ours into shape half as well as McClellan. If he can't fight himself, he excels in making others ready to fight."[123]

"But," one minister sputtered, "I cannot but feel that giving command back to McClellan is equivalent to giving Washington to the Rebels."[124]

Abraham replied, "Shall we receive the good at the hand of God, and not receive the bad?"[125] Each and all looked askance at their commander-in-chief, but he said with finality: "The order is mine, and I will be responsible for it to the country."[126]

---

[122] Job 1.21, *The New Oxford Annotated Bible*

[123] Lincoln, quoted in *The Civil War*, v. 2, pp. 648, 9

[124] Foote, *The Civil War*, v. 2, p. 649

[125] Job 2.10, *The New Oxford Annotated Bible*

[126] Lincoln, quoted in *The Civil War*, v. 2, p. 648

15 Defeatism was slowly creeping over the North.[127] Robert E. Lee, sensing as much, and hearing that George B. McClellan was back in command of the army of the North in the east, launched forth into Maryland, toward Washington, with fifty thousand fearless.

Frederick Douglass, the Runaway, expressed his frustration with the course of events: "I think the nation has never been more completely in the hands of the slave power.[128] Abraham Lincoln is no more fit for the place he holds than was his predecessor, and the latter was no more the miserable tool of traitors and Rebels than the former is allowing himself to be."[129]

But Little Mac was eager to answer his doubters, and he rushed out to meet the oncoming incursion; and, now, the Lord let slip into his hands the battle plans of Robert E. Lee. Thus George B. McClellan had all he needed to whip the Army of Northern Virginia, and maybe win the war, but instead he dithered, allowing Lee to change tactic and improvise a strong defensive position on high ground just short of a meandering rust-brown creek called Antietam.[130]

When George B. McClellan did finally attack, Lee's army doggedly held its ground, and the result was terrible: the bloodiest day in the nation's history, worse even than both days of Shiloh put together. Still, the Federals had many thousands in reserve, and if McClellan had pressed his advantage, the Rebel force might have been utterly destroyed, and maybe also

[127] McPherson, *The Negro's Civil War*, p. 48
[128] Douglass, quoted in *The Negro's Civil War*, p. 48
[129] Douglass, quoted in *The Negro's Civil War*, p. 47
[130] Foote, The Civil War, v. 2, p. 682

its cause. As was his wont, though, Little Mac found reasons for caution, even refusing to pursue Lee's retreating and fagged out troops at all. How many such opportunities had he squandered already? How many would he squander still? And why? The tactical victory of the North was by its own author erased, and the battle of Antietam now seemed merely tragic.

But Abraham Lincoln moved to generate a sense of momentum, himself. On September 22, 1862, not five days after Antietam, enacting a plan he had long had in place, Abraham Lincoln issued the Emancipation Proclamation, freeing all slaves in those states still in rebellion on the first of the following year. "All slaves in those states," he decreed, "would be then, thenceforward, and forever free."[131] Uncertain of the People's response to such a proclamation, Abraham announced it in a manner designed to cushion the shock, and to make it appear a necessary means of winning the war.[132]

But howsoever equivocal it was, the signal was clear enough, to both those who opposed and those who applauded it: the North was now fighting a war of liberation, for equality, and for basic human respect. And Frederick Douglass's despondency was suddenly transformed into elation:

> *"Free forever!*
> *O, long enslaved millions,*
> > *whose cries have so vexed the air and sky,*
> > > *suffer on a few more days in sorrow,*
> > > *the hour of your deliverance draws nigh!*

---

[131] McPherson, *Ordeal by Fire*, p. 292
[132] McPherson, *Ordeal by Fire*, p. 292

O, ye millions of free and loyal People,
who have earnestly sought to free your bleeding country
from the dreadful ravages of revolution and anarchy,
lift up now your voices with joy and thanksgiving
for with freedom to the slave
will come peace and safety to our country."[133]

Abraham Lincoln then met with George B. McClellan and fired him for the last time. God saw everything, heard everything, and indeed, she knew it was very good.[134]

16 But still the war went ill for the armies of the North. In the west, Ulysses S. Grant's army foundered, having their long extended supply lines continually cut by Nathan Bedford Forrest and others. William Tecumseh Sherman complained, "Though our armies pass across and through the land, the war closes in behind and leaves the same enemy behind. I don't see the end, or the beginning of the end."[135]

For him and Grant, and for Washington, and Richmond too, everything pivoted on Vicksburg, the city fortress on the Mississippi River, in the county called Ilium. Taking it would cut the South in half, rendering all friendly states and territories west of the Mississippi useless to the Confederacy. But the stronghold seemed impregnable, even unapproachable, a puzzle

---

[133] Douglass, quoted in *The Negro's Civil War*, p. 49
[134] Genesis 1.31, *The New Oxford Annotated Bible*
[135] Sherman, quoted in *The Civil War*, v. 1, p. 801

Ulysses might need ten more years to solve, and a million more men. Everything rested on that proud citadel, towering still,[136] and Ulysses S. Grant could not figure out how to get within its walls.

In the east, Union prospects were even grimmer as the incomparable Robert E. Lee, with the inestimable Stonewall Jackson, seemed to command every field. After dispatching George B. McClellan and all his loyalists, Abraham Lincoln appointed General Ambrose Burnside the commanding general of the whole army. But on December 14, 1862, a messenger came to Lincoln and reported: "Sir, General Burnside's Grand Divisions, three of two corps each, more than one hundred and twenty-one thousand effectives in all, further supported by eighty thousand more in reserve, faced Lee's army of a mere seventy-eight thousand, five hundred and eleven, and were summarily trounced.[137] It can hardly be human nature for men to show more valor, or generals to manifest less judgment, than were perceptible on our side yesterday.[138] They held the heights beyond Fredericksburg in Virginia, and our repeated attacks were ineffectual, to say the least. I alone from my brigade escaped to tell you."[139]

A month later, Abraham Lincoln replaced Ambrose Burnside with Fighting Joe Hooker, who had loudly claimed to be able to do much if only he could run all affairs. Lincoln gave him his chance, and then, on May 5, 1863, another messenger came to report to the president: "Sir, at

---

[136] Virgil, *The Aeneid*, p. 35

[137] Foote, *The Civil War*, v. 2, p. 21, 2

[138] Foote, *The Civil War*, v. 2, p. 44

[139] Job 1.16, *The New Oxford Annotated Bible*

Chancellorsville, Lee and Jackson turned the tables on us again, and very nearly annihilated our whole army. I still do not know how it happened, but it most certainly did. I alone, from my division, escaped to tell you."[140]

Abraham Lincoln walked up and down the room, hands clasped behind his back. "My God, my God," he exclaimed as he paced back and forth.[141] "Truly the thing that I fear most comes upon me, and what I dread befalls me."[142]

So it was when fifteen months earlier, the first of four messengers came to give him news he could never truly abide: "Your son, Willie, was eating and drinking, Sir, and suddenly a great sickness took him, and he is dead."[143] That day, Abraham Lincoln arose, tore his clothes, then fell to the ground, even in company.[144] By dawn the following day, though, he escaped his overwhelming grief to his official responsibilities. Mary Todd, his wife, distraught in equal measure, except that she was filled with jealous wrath for her husband's apparent fortitude— she snapped at him: "Do you still persist in your integrity? Curse God, and die."[145] And maybe he would have, but then the rising tide of the war demanded nothing less than all of him—and his reaction was less innate to him than merely necessary, like drawing breath, which he painfully did as he went about the People's business. But howsoever imperceptibly it manifest itself, his grief and resentment grew to such acuteness as Mary was only slightly more free to

---

[140] Job 1.17, *The New Oxford Annotated Bible*

[141] Foote, *The Civil War*, v. 2, p. 316

[142] Job 3.25, *The New Oxford Annotated Bible*

[143] Job 1.19, *The New Oxford Annotated Bible*

[144] Job 1.20, *The New Oxford Annotated Bible*

[145] Job 2.9, *The New Oxford Annotated Bible*

express, whether or not she knew it. "It is hard, hard to have him die,"[146] Abraham confessed to himself then.

Now, though, fifteen months later, the war effort he led by the guidance of his own heart appeared unambiguously futile, and that which buoyed him just barely before, seemed lost and gone. "Does it seem good to you to oppress, O Lord, to despise the work of your hands and favor the schemes of the wicked?"[147] he cried out. "Do you have eyes of flesh? Do you see as humans see?"[148] The frustration over his failures, and the grief over his son's death most of all, now flooded over him, and the ark of the Union did lurch inside Lincoln's chest. "O, let the day perish in which I was born. Let that day be darkness! Yes, let that night be barren; let no joyful cry be heard in it. Why did I not die at birth, come forth from the womb and expire? Why was I not buried like a stillborn child, like my late sister's infant that never saw the light and took hers from her as well?"[149]

And so the People cried too—all the People cried in Abraham's heart. In his heart, Abraham Lincoln felt all the People of the United States, North and South, and all the People of all the world, cry so; enemies, friends, heroes that were of old, warriors of renown,[150] and heroes never known, and never to be known, and everyone born in or through the singular chance of the ever present moment, and blind to all the chances outside it—humanity cried, he could feel it in his

---

[146] Lincoln, quoted in *Lincoln's Melancholy*, p. 178

[147] Job 10.3, *The New Oxford Annotated Bible*

[148] Job 10.5, *The New Oxford Annotated Bible*

[149] Job 3.3-4, 3.7, 3.11, and 3.16, *The New Oxford Annotated Bible*

[150] Genesis 6.4, *The New Oxford Annotated Bible*

heart, and despaired, like him, to have come to this great stage of fools.[151]

Harriet Tubman, a runaway slave who turned against every edict to free every other slave she could, believing in the strength of the immortal unrecorded laws of God,[152] and who was now looking upon the unfinished dome roof of the Capitol Building, suffering one of her recurring fevers[153]—she, perhaps more than anyone else, could sympathize:

> "S'pose dar was awfu' big snake down there, on de floor.
> He bite you.
> Folks all skeered, cause you die.
> You send for doctor to cut the bite;
> but snake he rolled up dar,
> and while doctor dwine it,
> he bite you agin.
> De doctor cut out dat bite;
> but while he dwine it,
> de snake he spring up and bite you agin,
> and so he keep dwine,
> agin and agin and agin.
> God's ahead ob Massa Linkum.
> Massa Linkum he a great man,
> and I'se poor nigger,
> but I understand."[154]

---

[151] Shakespeare, *King Lear*, IV. vi. 179, 80 (p. 1095)
[152] Sophocles, *Atigone*, p. 208
[153] Kendi, *Stamped from the Beginning*, p. 207
[154] Tubman, quoted in *The Negro's Civil War*, p. 43

And yet even in the very moment of such commiseration, the South's hope for foreign recognition and intervention was irreversibly crushed by emancipation; and so also did Ulysses S. Grant begin to turn over the solution to Vicksburg, in Ilium; and Robert E. Lee, intrepid as ever, did persuade Jefferson Davis to let him invade the North most fatefully.

And Thomas Jonathan Jackson, the Stonewall, hero of Chancellorsville, and of all the South, was dying. "Most men will think," he said luminously, "that I had planned the flank attack that crumbled and routed Fighting Joe; but it was not so. I simply took advantage of circumstances as they were presented to me in the providence of God. I feel that her hand led me."[155] His own men had shot him by mistake, in the dark, in the very moment of his greatest success in the war, and when he died, he died on a Sunday, of pneumonia, believing in the divine sanction of his purpose.

Dogma defeats its own reason. Wonder and humility are the only true piety, and gratitude, its greatest expression. The top-most glory of any experience is its spirit of tolerance—its broad human spirit of acceptance—its admission equally of every view—making dogma of none.[156]

 Now, there is a river in Tennessee called Stones. Running north to south, it branches from the arterial Cumberland east of Nashville, then pools, then forks, and forks again, near Murfreesboro, and forks beyond, and beyond

---

[156] Whitman, quoted in *Walt Whitman Speaks*, pp. 124, 5

again as into many capillaries. And astride one fork of the river Stones, just north of Murfreesboro, the Federal and Confederate armies bivouacked in opposing lines on the eve of battle, one night before Christmas Eve. The generals on their respective sides were planning bold assaults in the morning, and meanwhile their soldiers rested their bodies, and rallied their spirits the best they could in the mud and muck and wintry cold. And soon, the military bands on either side were compelled to answer every question. They played and the soldiers sang competing anthems: "Dixie" for the South, and "John Brown's Body" for the North, battling, defying, clashing discordance of the multiform pride of the People, louder and louder in the crisp night air hanging over the low hum of the river.

But spirits flagged, as spirits do, and relative silence swallowed both instrument and voice alike, just moments before tattoo.[157] Then it happened: one soldier named Caleb, and another called Joshua, in one band, on one side—no one knew from which—began to play "Home, Sweet Home," a song all the People knew, and that all People everywhere know; and soon the air was filled harmoniously with singing and bittersweet playing on both sides of the crooked dividing line.[158] The chorus runs:

> *"Home! Home!*
> *Sweet, sweet home!*
> *There's no place like home.*
> *There's no place like home."*

---

[157] Foote, *The Civil War*, v. 2. p. 86
[158] Numbers 14.6, *The New Oxford Annotated Bible*

The song ended, as songs do, but from completion this time, not exhaustion. Silence ensued again, but deeper than the one before; and there was not a single soldier anywhere who was not awed by what just happened, like a miracle arisen from inside each of them, there where the Stones flows north to south above Murfreesboro. A soldier might have wondered, "But are we not one family, one People, all of us children of the Lord, our God—all of us her chosen ones?"[159] Does not the ache for home live in all of us?"[160]

And the Lord answers inaudibly,

"So it is the whole world over, and so it shall ever be . . .
Not words, not music or rhyme I want,
    not custom or lecture,
        not even the best.
Out of the dimness opposite equals advance,
    always substance and increase,
    always a knit of identity,
    always distinction,
    always a breed of life.
Urge and urge and urge,
    always the procreant urge of the world.
Showing the best and dividing it from the worst,
    age vexes age.
O I wish I could translate
    the hints about the dead young men and women,
        and the hints about old men and mothers,
    and the offspring taken soon out of their laps.[161]

---

[159] Deuteronomy 14.1-2, *The New Oxford Annotated Bible*
[160] Angelou, *All God's Children Need Traveling Shoes*
[161] Whitman, *Leaves of Grass* (1855), pg. 30, 28-9, 32

Howsoever much your tongues are confused, my People,
your hearts should never be.
I am the Lord, your God, the God of the United States,
and I say,
Your real country is where you are heading,
not where you are."[162]

And that night, December 30th, became every night of the whole war, and becomes every night of every war the world over, in all of human history. Before the Battle of Murfreesboro, through all too much imperfection, a glimpse of the original, natural design—the national design amazed all, and rendered all dumb. But the opposing generals, unawares, wrote and sent their orders, and both planned to attack on the right in the morning, and like a drill they might could spin around each other and bore into the earth a hundred miles deep, and dig a hole to collect the senseless immolation. Inside their hearts, the soldiers of the two armies ached, and they all wept that night.[163]

Yet there is divinity in docility, too, a righteous truth to simpleness. That the meek may be exploited misses their worth completely. Gullibility betrays honesty, and betrays the evaluation of life upon which a person could do no better than to settle. Let all of those on the earth learn to love what grows from it: let them learn to love and seek that equilibrium which is its own greatest ideal—to seek it in themselves. Leadership is either worthy of humility, from river to creek to merest tributary, or it is none.

---

[162] Rumi, *The Essential Rumi*
[163] Numbers 14.1, *The New Oxford Annotated Bible*

IV

18 Robert E. Lee, the noble aristocrat, favored of God so highly, the Old Virginian, who would never have presumed to own another human being, but who could not ultimately bring himself to fight against the People of his own State—Robert E. Lee, the great strategist, who did not merely anticipate, much less react to his enemy's movements, but who forced them, as if the whole field were his own—yes, Robert E. Lee, the venerable commander who wrought the Army of Northern Virginia in his own image[164]—he was sensing the fierce urgency of now.[165] It was not the loss of Stonewall that stirred him. The simple fact was that against so vastly superior a force, Stonewall or no, the hope for terms such as the South could dictate was always dwindling, by every minute of every hour of every day. Already Ulysses S. Grant, the indefatigable commander of the army of the North in the west, had found the foothold he needed to take Vicksburg. Forty days more, and that last stitch holding the South together would be overthrown.[166]

But even more pressing on Lee was the supreme confidence his own army had won after the string of so many total victories since Antietam. The morale of his troops brimmed even as did their direst need for it, he felt. The Confederacy's best chance had come. Its moment was now. "Follow after me," he told his soldiers, "for the Lord has given

---

[164] Genesis 1.26, *The New Oxford Annotated Bible*

[165] Martin Luther King Jr., "I Have a Dream"

[166] Jonah 3.4, *The New Oxford Annotated Bible*

your enemies into your hand."[167] And he did not have to force
himself to believe what he said.

Frederick Douglass, in the North, grew impatient as well.
The threat posed by Lee's army was existential for the cause of
his life, of course, and yet Lincoln's government was slow to
ask for the help of those who had most at stake—slow to ask the
Blacks to fight—slow to believe they could.

> *"If persons so humble as we*
> *can be allowed to speak*
> *to the President of the United States,*
> *we should ask him if this dark and terrible hour*
> *of the nation's extremity is a time for consulting*
> *a mere vulgar and unnatural prejudice?*
>
> *While the Government continues to refuse*
> *the aid of colored men,*
> *thus alienating them from the national cause,*
> *it will not deserve better fortunes*
> *than it has thus far experienced.*[168]
>
> *Colored men were good enough*
> *to fight under Washington.*
> *They were good enough*
> *to fight under Andrew Jackson.*
> *They were good enough*
> *to help win American independence,*

---

[167] Judges 3.28, *The New Oxford Annotated Bible*
[168] Douglass, quoted in *The Negro's Civil War*, p. 164

but are they not good enough
to help preserve that independence
against treason and rebellion?[169]

Men in earnest, do not fight with one hand,
when they might fight with two,
and a man drowning
would not refuse to be saved
even by a colored hand."[170]

And sure enough, Abraham Lincoln, the President of the United States of America, did promise to grant Frederick Douglass audience in the White House when the next chance arose. Douglass thought to himself:

"Once let the Black man
get upon his person
the brass letters, U.S.,
let him get an eagle on his button,
and a musket on his shoulder
and bullets in his pocket,
and there is no power on earth
which can deny that he has earned
the right to citizenship."[171]

---

[169] Douglass, quoted in *The Negro's Civil War*, p. 165
[170] Douglass, quoted in *The Negro's Civil War*, p. 164
[171] Douglass, quoted in *The Negro's Civil War*, p. 163

19 In the west, Ulysses S. Grant was become a name.[172] "In positions of great responsibility," he stated his orthodoxy, "every one should do his duty to the best of his ability where assigned by competent authority, without application of the use of influence to change his position."[173] But what appeared as determination, or even stubbornness to his allies, appeared as guile, envy, and ruthlessness to his enemies.[174] He and the army of the North pressed the army of the South into the hill country; they did not allow them to come down to the plain.[175]

But Ulysses was far from certain of success, even now. Repeated assaults on Vicksburg proved worse than fruitless, bolstering the resolve of its defenders and inhabitants. His task: to block all attempts at relief or reinforcement of Vicksburg while he starved its defenders into submission. But to do this he had to subsist his own army without being made vulnerable by Forrest's slashing raids on his supply lines. The latter was the key, and he had figured it out, at last—it was his masterstroke: brutal as it did appear to be and was to the People of Ilium, he learned how to convert their bounty systematically into his provision.

But Johnston the Lesser, Joseph Egglesworth Johnston, recently rehabilitated to command per necessity for the South, was rumored to have cobbled together some thirty thousand effectives to try to throw off the siege and rescue Vicksburg.

---

[172] Tennyson, "Ulysses", *The Norton Anthology of Poetry*, p. 992

[173] Grant, *The Personal Memoirs*, p. 318

[174] Virgil, *The Aeneid*, p. 122

[175] Judges 1.34, *The New Oxford Annotated Bible*

He posed no serious threat to Grant and Sherman's forces, except that he did encourage the garrison at Vicksburg to hold out hope for his coming. Time thus became the sole question of Grant's campaign, and of the war.

Robert E. Lee and the Army of Northern Virginia were invading the North, and with a victory over the Union army in the east, which by then seemed as much a likelihood to Grant as it did to everyone else, they might very well force Grant's army to abandon the siege, and rush to Washington's defense. What havoc could Johnston and Nathan Bedford Forrest cause him then? No, Ulysses S. Grant was far from certain of success, though he also never seemed susceptible to concern over the vagaries of war, or even of his own second guesses. "He habitually wears an expression," one of his fellows said of him, "as if he had determined to drive his head through a brick wall, and was about to do it."[176] Ulysses S. Grant was become a name. [177]

Abraham Lincoln was, contrarily, far more subject to his fortunes, and more desperate of them, and he, at last, resigned himself to put his trust where he could not think to put it. One night, he had a dream in which he was standing on a boat, and the waters increased, and bore up the boat, high above the earth. The waters swelled so mightily on the earth that all the high mountains under the whole heaven were covered. And all flesh died that moved on the earth—birds, domestic animals, wild animals, all swarming creatures, and all human beings, the North, and the South, and the many nations connected by land, and those once separated by seas, and every person of every

[176] Foote, *The Civil War*, v. 1, p. 5
[177] Tennyson, "Ulysses", *The Norton Anthology of Poetry*, p. 992

kind, and color, and creed, all died. They were blotted out.[178]
And he, himself, was blotted out, too. He was no longer a
person at all, not a father, nor a husband, nor even a president,
but was only part of the boat, part of the nation that was now
little more than flotsam and debris. Its sodden banner of the
Union, of the once proud People of the United States, was
wrapped so tightly about its staff, so fearfully clinging to its
pole, that even when the rain subsided, and a wind started to
blow across it, it could not, and did not stir.[179]

Waking from this dream, Abraham accepted the
resignation of Fighting Joe Hooker, then surprised himself and
met with an equally surprised George Gordon Meade, third in
line for the position, looking more like a learned pundit than a
soldier.[180] Abraham Lincoln said in their meeting, "God's will
be done. I am in her hands."[181] Meade did not know how to
respond, and, indeed, Lincoln did not look at him, but looked
beyond him, out the window, speaking as if he were alone, as if
into a mirror. "In great contests each party claims to act in
accordance with the will of God. Both may be, and one must
be wrong." Meade tried to follow, but Lincoln pressed
obliviously, methodically on: "You see, in the present civil war
it is quite possible that God's purpose is something different
from the purpose of either party."[182] Still Meade remained
silent, but then the president's eyes fell upon him almost with a
thud. "We must work earnestly in the best light she gives us,

[178] Genesis 7.17-23, *The New Oxford Annotated Bible*
[179] Genesis 8.1, *The New Oxford Annotated Bible*
[180] Foote, *The Civil War*, v. 2, p. 454
[181] Lincoln, quoted in *Lincoln's Melancholy*, p. 197
[182] Lincoln, quoted in *Lincoln's Melancholy*, p. 198

George, trusting that so working still conduces to the great ends she ordains.[183] You must do all you possibly can."

And even thus was George Gordon Meade, third in line for the position, placed in full command of the army of the North in the east, while Lee's vaunted army foraged and gained momentum somewhere behind the Alleghenies of Pennsylvania.

20 In the eighty seventh year of the Union, in the seventh month, the first day of the month,[184] early in the morning, an infantry brigade from Lee's army went to seize shoes rumored to have been stored for the army of the North in a quiet, little town in western Pennsylvania called Gettysburg. That brigade clashed with two scouting cavalry brigades of Bluecoats. Neither army had planned to fight in this place, nor was it prepared to do so, but the strategic importance of the town quickly became obvious once the battle began: a dozen roads converged from every point on the compass right there, enabling a speedy concentration and deployment of both forces.[185] Like a great whirlpool, the simple, little truth of Gettysburg drew the crux of everything toward itself.

Unaware of either enemy's position or total strength, and disorganized themselves, both armies were surprised by the increasing intensity of the fighting, and by the early ebb and

---

[183] Lincoln, quoted in *Lincoln's Melancholy*, p. 199
[184] Genesis 8.13, *The New Oxford Annotated Bible*
[185] McPherson, *Ordeal by Fire*, p. 324

flow of success on the darkling plain.[186]　Robert E. Lee's army, though, was able to achieve a faster concentration, and it eventually pushed the army of the North south of the town, up onto two linked hills called Cemetery and Culp's.[187]　On the cemetery gate of Cemetery Hill there was a sign that read: "All persons found using firearms in these grounds will be prosecuted with the utmost rigor of the law."[188]

Still unsure of what was happening, or of what had already happened, Lee gave a discretionary order to his general on site—the same general who had replaced Stonewall Jackson: "Take the hill if practicable."[189]　But the commander, in general shock and wonder, himself, and tuckered out by so long a day of such suspense, hesitated.　And thus, by the end of the following night, any advantage the Rebels held by surprise was lost, and the great bulk of the Union army had arrived and taken strong defensive positions all along the higher ground south of the city.　Robert E. Lee and George Gordon Meade, not sure exactly how it happened, now saw in one another the destined end of all their blind stumbling.

In the morning, July 2, 1863, Robert E. Lee said to his soldiers, "The Lord, the God of America, commands you, 'Go, take position on that mount, bringing seventy-two thousand with you!'"[190]　They all shouted in reply, "A sword for the Lord and for Robert E. Lee!"[191] and they attacked right and left of center with much vigor and belief.　On the far right, in

---

[186] Arnold, "Dover Beach", The Norton Anthology of Poetry, p. 1101

[187] McPherson, *Ordeal by Fire*, p. 324

[188] McPherson, *Ordeal by Fire*, p. 324

[189] Lee, quoted in *Ordeal by Fire*, p. 324

[190] Judges 4.6, *The New Oxford Annotated Bible*

[191] Judges 7.20, *The New Oxford Annotated Bible*

particular, on a steeper ground called Little Round Top, not yet well-guarded, and overlooking the entire Union position, the Confederates very nearly achieved everything Lee could hope for. But a last-chance countercharge by the 20th of Maine, such a charge as was reminiscent of Stonewall himself, thwarted and threw back the Gray tide of war. The Rebels were repulsed with heavy casualties, and the strangeness of defeat in contrast with such high hopes—with such sure belief, left some to wonder, "Did the Lord change her mind about the disaster she planned to bring the North?"[192]

That night, the Army of Northern Virginia inquired of Robert E. Lee, "Shall we again draw near to battle against our kinfolk?" And Robert E. Lee replied, "Go up against them." And by midday, July 3, 1863, they took courage and again formed the battle line.[193] They yelled, "March on, my soul, with might!"[194] And they marched with such zeal, and in so grand a spectacle, that no charge of the war would ever equal it in memory or legacy. They charged the stoutly defended center, atop the ridge of Cemetery Hill, where it was expressly forbidden to use firearms. They charged with great hope and confidence, and they were slaughtered.

By the end of the battle, closing with this third assault on the third day, the Federal army had suffered nearly as many casualties as the Confederates: twenty-four thousand soldiers each, in the bloodiest battle of the war, far surpassing both Shiloh and Antietam. But twenty-four thousand soldiers was nearly a full third of the entire Army of Northern Virginia, and

---

[192] Exodus 32.14, *The New Oxford Annotated Bible*
[193] Judges 20.21, *The New Oxford Annotated Bible*
[194] Judges 5.21, *The New Oxford Annotated Bible*

at this stage of the war, in an attempt as desperate as it was bold, it was a loss the South could scarcely sustain. And greater defeat, even a complete surrender, seemed likely. Recent rains bulged the Potomac River, making it unfordable, cutting off Lee's only path of retreat.[195] He said to his army, "It's all my fault, all my fault...[196] Perhaps, though," he prayed, "the Lord will spare us a thought so we do not all perish."[197]

George Gordon Meade, unaware of the extent of his advantage, and despite being directly ordered by Lincoln to attack with his rested reserves, he refused to do so, in either an excessiveness of caution or personal fatigue. "We have them in our grasp!" Lincoln exclaimed. "We have only to stretch forth our hands and they are ours."[198]   But Robert E. Lee and his vaunted army escaped to fight another day.

21 The 4th of July.   It is yearly called Independence Day in these United States. The Lord, the God of America, says, "This day shall be a day of remembrance for the People.   You shall celebrate it as a festival to the Lord; throughout your generations you shall observe it as a perpetual ordinance."[199]   And on July 4, 1863, suspecting he might win better terms of surrender on this day, General Pemberton Priam of Pennsylvania, who, siding with his wife's family from Virginia from the outset of the war, was now

---

[195] McPherson, *Ordeal by Fire*, p. 329
[196] Lee, quoted in *Ordeal by Fire*, p. 329
[197] Jonah 1.6, *The New Oxford Annotated Bible*
[198] Lincoln, quoted in *Ordeal by Fire*, p. 330
[199] Exodus 12.14, *The New Oxford Annotated Bible*

commanding the redoubtable garrison of Graycoats at Vicksburg, came through Union lines under a flag of truce to meet with General Grant.

His command informed him a few nights before, by way of a letter signed "Many Soldiers," that they could not hold out against hunger any longer. "The emergency of the case demands prompt and decided action: if you can't feed us, you had better surrender us, horrible as the idea is, than suffer this noble army to disgrace themselves by desertion."[200]   And Johnston the Lesser, with his scratch unit behind Grant's lines, much to the disgust of Jefferson Davis in Richmond, stated the obvious, "I am too weak to save Vicksburg.[201]   I consider any attempt to do so hopeless."[202]

Pemberton Priam formally surrendered what was left of the army of the South in the west on July 4th, 1863, one day after Lee's retreat from Gettysburg. Neither Pemberton, nor Ulysses knew of the developments in the east, but in Richmond, Jeff Davis's left eye percolated with rage over the double reversal of his fortunes.

The Vicksburg campaign, after much anxiety and delay, was a total success for Ulysses S. Grant. With fewer than ten thousand casualties of his own, he inflicted as many on his foe, but then captured thirty-seven thousand more.[203]   William Tecumseh Sherman spoke roundly about his opponent, "You have not obeyed the command of the Lord. You are not to have treated any of the People as you have treated the Blacks.

---

[200] Foote, *The Civil War*, v. 2, p. 415

[201] Johnston, quoted in *The Civil War*, v. 2, p. 413

[202] Johnston, quoted in *Ordeal by Fire*, p. 330

[203] McPherson, *Ordeal by Fire*, p. 330

See what you have done! The Blacks shall not suffer your ordinances any longer, but they shall become adversaries to you, and a snare."[204] But Ulysses S. Grant showed what might have seemed uncharacteristic of him by then: clemency. He paroled the prisoners, and said,

> *"The Lord is a God*
> *merciful and gracious,*
> *slow to anger,*
> *and abounding in steadfast love*
> *   and faithfulness,*
> *keeping steadfast love to the last generation,*
> *forgiving iniquity and transgression and sin."*[205]

Abraham Lincoln, on hearing the news of this, said, "Grant is my man, and I am his the rest of the war.[206] For he has been as one suffering all that suffers nothing, a man that Fortune's buffets and rewards has taken with equal thanks. Give me that man that is not passion's slave, and I will wear him in my heart's core, ay, in my heart of heart."[207]

He bid Ulysses to leave his army in the west, and to make his way up to take command of the army in the east, and to try and subdue Robert E. Lee. William Tecumseh Sherman was to supply his former command, and do whatever he and Ulysses thought best. Thus, General Ulysses S. Grant became a lieutenant-general, the likes of which honor had not been conferred on anyone other than George Washington himself.

---

[204] Judges 2.3, *The New Oxford Annotated Bible*

[205] Exodus 34.6-7, *The New Oxford Annotated Bible*

[206] Lincoln, quoted in *Ordeal by Fire*, p. 332

[207] Shakespeare, *Hamlet*, III. ii. 62-70 (p. 952)

Imagining Grant possessed precisely what he, himself, lacked and needed most, Abraham Lincoln gave him complete command of all forces of the North.

A dove then came to Lincoln's window, and there in its beak was a freshly plucked olive leaf.[208] Abraham crept up to the window, and opened it. The dove flew away, and Lincoln followed it with his eyes. Then he felt the warming air, like a smile upon his face, and he thought of the Lord, the God of the United States, and picked up the olive leaf.

22 Frederick Douglass, a month later, was received at the White House. "May the Lord reward you for your deeds," Abraham Lincoln greeted him, "and may you have a full reward from the Lord, the God of the United States, under whose wings you have come for refuge."[209]

"What deeds?" Frederick Douglass asked, almost curtly. "What refuge do I seek?"

Abraham Lincoln looked quizzically at the slave who would not hide in the shadows—the slave who would not even just lower his head.[210]

Frederick Douglass then started:

---

[208] Genesis 8.11, *The New Oxford Annotated Bible*
[209] Ruth 2.12, *The New Oxford Annotated Bible*
[210] Job 7.2, *The New Oxford Annotated Bible*

"Where you go, I will go, Mr. President;
    where you lodge, I will lodge;
I am counted among the People,
    and your God is my God.

Where you die, and how, I will die, too—
    there and in that way I will be buried.
May the Lord do thus and so to me,
    and to mine own,
    and do more as well,
        praised be the Lord."[211]

Lincoln's brow tightened in solemn concentration. He could see, on the instant, that Douglass suffered all the chances of the war even more than he, much more, in a way he could scarcely understand—in an arena both defining the present moment and extending infinitely beyond it. Yes, beyond his own tenuous beginnings, and his political life, and hopes— beyond his own all-consuming utility, and that of his generals and armies, and even beyond Douglass's own valiant efforts, well beyond his brand of assimilationism, in a country whose departure from perfection on the question of equality was from its inception grossly iniquitous, and more grossly countenanced, Lincoln could newly see the struggle for respect and just treatment of all God's People far outstretching his own calculations. In that weathered brow of his countryman, Lincoln could see the endless courage of those who fought off and slipped away from their captors on their own, and who ran to freedom on their own—who had fought for life and dignity in the worse conditions imaginable, and who would fight now

---

[211] Ruth 1.16-17, *The New Oxford Annotated Bible*

and forever to align the nation's promise and claims to greatness with a true reckoning and redress of its constitutional sin.[212]

"We hold these truths to—to be self-evi—dent, that—" Lincoln stammered, then let the sound of his voice fall off. He offered Douglass a seat, then took his own, and started again,

> *"Surely one does not turn against the needy,*
> *when in disaster they cry for help.[213]*
> *If I have raised my hand against the orphan,*
> *because I saw I had supporters at the gate;*
> *then let my shoulder blade fall from my shoulder,*
> *and let my arm be broken from its socket."[214]*

But before Frederick could reply, Abraham stretched out his hand with his arm turning in its socket,[215] pleading for patience:

> *"Did not she who made me in the womb make thee?*
> *Did not she fashion us in the womb of the earth?[216]*
> *Injustice anywhere*
> *is a threat to justice everywhere.[217]*
> *That is a definitively American ideal,*
> *is it not?"*

---

[212] Kendi, *Stamped from the Beginning*, p. 227

[213] Job 30.24, *The New Oxford Annotated Bible*

[214] Job 31.21-22, *The New Oxford Annotated Bible*

[215] Exodus 14.21, *The New Oxford Annotated Bible*

[216] Job 31.15, *The New Oxford Annotated Bible*

[217] Martin Luther King Jr., "Letter from Birmingham Jail" (1963)

Douglass smiled, and Lincoln mirrored it, then said:

> *"We are caught*
> *in an inescapable network of mutuality,*
> *tied in a single garment of destiny.*[218]

> *There will be some black men, indeed, Frederick,*
> *who can remember that,*
> *with silent tongue, and clenched teeth,*
> *with steady eye, and well-poised bayonet,*
> *they have helped mankind on to this great consummation."*[219]

Douglass breathed in resonantly, then rose from his seat, and the president did, too. There was to be no legal difference between Black soldiers and White, nor between any and all who would come and strive to help perfect the Union of the United States of America. The two men looked evenly into each other's eyes.

> *"The utmost reward of daring should be still to dare."*[220]

Abraham Lincoln led his guest to the door, then stopped and shook his hand firmly. Frederick Douglass turned directly, and walked out into the sunlight, having rolled up his sleeves before descending the first stair.

But by the time Abraham returned to his office, his resolute demeanor had dropped off completely, like a mask, and he said to himself, "I also fear there will be some White men, unable to forget that, with malignant heart, and deceitful speech, they

---

[218] Martin Luther King Jr., "Letter from a Birmingham Jail" (1963)

[219] Lincoln, quoted in *Ordeal by Fire*, p. 196

[220] Frost, "Trial by Existence", *Frost*, p.28

have strove to hinder such consummation as we now enact."[221]
Looming large in his mind, more menacingly than ever before,
was the fact that in little more than a year, he would be up for
re-election, and he trembled to think what would happen if he
lost that race before the war could be won.

Mary Todd, his wife, came into his quarters, saw his empty,
overwhelmed expression, and was startled by it—affliction even
greater than her unabating own, right when she imagined his
resources to have been replenished and available. Putting her
own purposes aside for the moment, she managed
unconvincingly to plead with him to take better care of
himself.

His stare was devoid of life, his eyes like fallen stars, like
cold stones in the craters of their own exhaustion. "I have been
charged with so vast, so sacred a trust," he said, "that I feel I
have no moral right to shrink, nor even to count the chances of
my own life, in what might follow."[222] She remained silent,
and fearful, and she watched him walk to the other side of the
room, away from her, as if bearing too great a weight. Facing
the wall where he stood, he summoned a voice, "God's will be
done. I am in her hands."[223] Then he turned, and regarded his
wife again.

Was it the hint of a smile that creased his lips then, or
did she simply need it to be?

"Mary," he permitted himself, "I shall be most happy
indeed if I shall be a humble instrument in the hands of the

---

[221] Lincoln, quoted in *Ordeal by Fire*, p. 196

[222] Lincoln, quoted in *Lincoln's Melancholy*, p. 197

[223] Lincoln, quoted in *Lincoln's Melancholy*, p. 197

Lord, our God, and of this, her almost chosen People, for perpetuating the object of this great struggle."[224]

23

After the battle of Gettysburg, the project of burying the dead became a major public work.[225] Edward Everett, the Harvard president, and U.S. senator, and celebrated orator, who once thought Lincoln wholly unequal to the crisis, was asked to give the keynote address at the dedication ceremony of the new national cemetery in that place where firearms were strictly prohibited.[226] Abraham Lincoln was asked merely for "a few appropriate remarks," which invitation he did also accept.[227]

Thursday, November 19, 1863, on the grounds of Gettysburg, Edward Everett delivered a speech about two hours in length, and after much applause, he ceded the rostrum to the president. Abraham Lincoln rose, and spoke for hardly two minutes. A smattering of applause, in astonishment of one kind or another, followed him back to his seat. He felt he had failed the moment.

But this is what he had said:

> "*Four score and seven years ago*
> *our fathers brought forth on this continent,*
> *a new nation,*
> *conceived in liberty,*

[224] Lincoln, quoted in *Lincoln's Melancholy*, p. 198

[225] Shenk, *Lincoln's Melancholy*, p. 200

[226] Shenk, *Lincoln's Melancholy*, p. 172

[227] Shenk, *Lincoln's Melancholy*, p. 200

and dedicated to the proposition
that all are created equal.

Now we are engaged in a great civil war,
testing whether that nation,
or any nation so conceived
and so dedicated,
can long endure.

We are met on a great battlefield of that war.
We have come to dedicate a portion of that field,
as a final resting place
for those who here gave their lives
that that nation might live.

It is altogether fitting and proper
that we should do this.
But, in a larger sense,
we can not dedicate—
we can not consecrate—
we can not hallow this ground.
The brave men, living and dead,
who struggled here,
have consecrated it far above our poor power
to add or detract.

The world will little note
nor long remember what we say here,
but it can never forget what they did here.

It is for us the living, rather,
to be dedicated here to the unfinished work
which they who fought here

have thus far so nobly advanced.

It is rather for us to be here dedicated
to the great task remaining before us—
that from these honored dead
we take increased devotion to that cause
for which they gave the last full measure of devotion—
that we here highly resolve that these dead
shall not have died in vain—
that this nation, under God,
shall have a new birth of freedom—
and that government of the People,
by the People,
for the People,
shall not perish from the earth."228

Edward Everett, whose curiosity and intelligence were always highly engaged, was not sure exactly what he had just heard, but he could sense the magnitude of its effect, rifling down through the ages. "I should be glad," he later wrote to Lincoln, "if I could flatter myself that I came as near to the central idea of the occasion, in two hours, as you did in two minutes.[229] Those words should be inscribed in a book, or better yet, with an iron pen and with lead, they should be engraved on a rock forever!"[230]

---

[228] Lincoln, "Gettysburg Address", as printed in *Lincoln's Melancholy*
[229] Everett, quoted in *The Civil War*, v. 2, p. 833
[230] Job 19.23-24, *The New Oxford Annotated Bible*

V

24

Near the close of the year 1863, after hearing of yet another stinging defeat at the hands of Grant, and really, even worse, at the hands of pure luck, there in his cavernous office in Richmond, Jefferson Davis dropped a load of dry boughs to stoke his fire. He poked the fire, heaping on brushwood.[231] Robert E. Lee knocked on his door and entered. Jefferson Davis wheeled all the way around to look at him with his one good eye. "We are now in the darkest hour of our political existence,"[232] Davis said with something of a huff, then he stood and walked methodically to his desk.

"We must expect reverses, even defeats," Lee responded. "They are sent to teach us wisdom and prudence, to call forth greater energies, and to prevent our falling into greater disasters. Our People have only to be true and united, and all will come right in the end."[233]

Davis tilted his head, trying to better discern his star general's condition. "I have felt more than ever before the want of your advice, Robert. Misfortune often develops secret foes." He sat carefully, using both his hands to assure himself of his chair. "Even Old Edmund Ruffin, who carries the first shot of the war like a trophy in his mouth—even he has turned against me."[234]

Lee took his seat as well, but sat stiffly. "You know how prone we are to censure," he said. "You know how ready we

---

[231] Homer, *The Odyssey*, p. 152

[232] Davis, quoted in *The Civil War*, v. 2, p. 642

[233] Lee, quoted in *The Civil War*, v. 2, p. 656

[234] Davis, quoted in *The Civil War*, v. 2, pp. 647, 8

are to blame others for the non-fulfillment of our expectations. This is unbecoming in a generous People, and I grieve to see its expression.[235] But do not give heed to everything that People say."[236]

"Did you hear of Chattanooga?" Davis asked.

Lee nodded. "Missionary Ridge was a clear blunder."

"And have you heard the 'conciliatory' remarks from Washington? From that despot? That man who would hold to principles only so long as he had more to gain than lose by them. Slippery. Mendacious. Contemptible![237] I would I could take both Lincoln and U.S. Grant into my hands and beat their brains out."[238] Davis stilled the tumult rising inside him, then exhaled: "Vengeance will be our motto."[239]

Robert E. Lee shifted slightly in his seat, trying to sit even more upright than before. "I request Your Excellency to take measures to supply my place."[240]

Jefferson Davis could not believe what he just heard.

Lee continued: "I do this with the more earnestness because no one is more aware than my self of my inability for the duties of my position. Everything points to the advantages to be

---

[235] Lee, quoted in *The Civil War*, v. 2, p. 657

[236] Ecclesiastes 7.21, *The New Oxford Annotated Bible*

[237] Davis, quoted in *The Civil War*, v. 2, p. 883

[238] Homer, *The Odyssey*, p. 153

[239] McPherson, *For Cause & Comrades*, p.149

[240] Lee, quoted in *The Civil War*, v. 2, p. 657

derived from a new commander, one younger and abler than myself."[241]

After a pause, Davis mumbled, "The clouds are truly dark over us."[242] Then with both sympathy and astonishment, he said very carefully, "Sir, to ask me to substitute you by someone in my judgment more fit to command, or who could possess more of the confidence of the army or of the more reflecting People in the country, is to demand of me an impossibility."[243]

But Lee asserted himself, "I have been prompted, Sir, by my own reflections since my return from Pennsylvania to propose to Your Excellency the propriety of selecting another commander for this army.[244] It is better that one should not vow than that one should vow and not fulfill it."[245]

Jefferson Davis then stood and took a moment to balance himself. Like the soldier he was, Lee stood as well. Jefferson spoke: "There is a reliable hope for peace in the vigor of our resistance. The cessation of hostility from the People of the North is to be expected from the pressure of their necessities.[246] There is no one better than you to execute our will. Resist, and in less than a year, Lincoln will be removed from office, and replaced by another who will win the presidency on a platform for peace and proper social structure. There is hope, General," Jefferson Davis said, "there is hope for you and for me."

---

[241] Lee, quoted in *The Civil War*, v. 2, p. 657

[242] Davis, quoted in *The Civil War*, v. 2, p. 644

[243] Davis, quoted in *The Civil War*, v. 2, p. 657

[244] Lee, quoted in *The Civil War*, v. 2, p. 657

[245] Ecclesiastes 5.5, *The New Oxford Annotated Bible*

[246] Davis, quoted in *The Civil War*, v. 2, p. 879

"Not a whit," Lee thought to himself on the instant. But he saluted the president of the Confederate States of America, in that large, echoing chamber of an office in Richmond. Still, in his head, and in his heart, Lee said, "We defy augury.[247] If a person is meant to die on land, he will not drown. If death on the battlefield is to be his lot, he will not die in the cradle. God's dispositions are wise and her ways are inscrutable.[248] The readiness is all."[249] He was looking out the window, but he brought his eyes back to Jeff's, first drawn to the diseased mess of his left, but quickly shifting and settling on the right. Then he said aloud, "Let be."[250] Robert E. Lee dismissed himself, and left Jefferson Davis standing in perplexity.

25 In the first week of May, 1864, Ulysses S. Grant, now directly commanding the army of the North in the east, and William Tecumseh Sherman, now at the head of the army of the North in the west, both launched forth to conquer a peace. But whatever fortune assisted them together six months earlier at Chattanooga, it now seemed to have abandoned both separately.

Robert E. Lee selected to attack Grant's oncoming Bluecoats in the Wilderness south of the Rapidan River, not far from Chancellorsville, where he and Stonewall had won so decisively almost exactly a year before. But Grant, so much

---

[247] Shakespeare, *Hamlet*, V. ii. 208 (p. 971)

[248] Catton, *A Stillness at Appomattox*, p. 217

[249] Shakespeare, *Hamlet*, V. ii. 211 (p. 971)

[250] Shakespeare, *Hamlet*, V. ii. 212, 3 (p. 971)

more aggressive and determined than any of his predecessors, very nearly crushed Lee on the right, pushing the Rebels back even to Lee's own headquarters. Reinforcements, General Longstreet's division of Texans, arrived on the instant, but Lee was already committed to charge, himself, most recklessly. He called out,

> *"Vindicate me, O Lord,*
>   *for I have walked in my integrity,*
> *and I have trusted in the Lord*
>   *without wavering.*
> *Prove me, O Lord, and try me;*
>   *test my heart and mind."*[251]

He reared up on his horse, and was about to lead a desperate, final countercharge, when the newly arrived troops shouted, "General Lee to the rear."[252] And a few soldiers even seized his horse and led him away. Longstreet's counterattack, coming just in time, shocked the Yankees, and recovered from them all the ground and confidence they had earlier taken. By close of day, the two camps, North and South, Union and Rebel, started to entrench for a protracted battle. And so Lee had maintained his defensive advantage.

Ulysses S. Grant, so accustomed to victory himself, and again so near to it here, was shaken as never before. The surrounding woods caught on fire during the fighting, and now the death-cries of the wounded rang in his ears. It was horrible, and he could find no rest that night, even as after the first night of Shiloh. But on the morn two days later, both the

---

[251] Psalms 26.1-2, *The New Oxford Annotated Bible*
[252] McPherson, *Ordeal by Fire*, p. 416

Army of Northern Virginia and the army of the North were equally surprised. Grant's army was on the move, but not back to where it started—not back to Washington, as all had come to expect. No, it left the entrenchments early, sidestepped the enemy, and then continued on toward Richmond. Grant, himself, atop his horse, led his soldiers forward, and all of a moment the tired column of soldiers came alive, and a wild cheer broke out.[253] The Bluecoats had just been through hell, in a battle not much unlike Chancellorsville, and the move southward promised only more of the same, and likely worse, much worse, but Ulysses S. Grant would not turn back, and that fact alone gave his army a strange sense of victory.[254]

 Robert E. Lee, as surprised as any, nevertheless saw Grant's next move, and so it was a race, then, to Spotsylvania, and Lee won it—just barely. The Federals broke the Confederate line twice, but could not sustain it either time, and another stalemate seemed likely to ensue.

But Ulysses S. Grant ordered another long flanking movement. He hoped to get between Lee and Richmond, but it depended on beating Lee to the punch, which lacking the interior line, familiarity of the land, and most significantly a smaller army, he could not manage to do. But Grant was nothing if not determined, and he tried again and again, until his soldiers were physically spent.

---

[253] Catton, *A Stillness at Appomattox*, p. 92

[254] McPherson, *Ordeal by Fire*, p. 418

On June 3, 1864, Ulysses S. Grant's frustration with all his limitations, some natural, some bumbling, led him to a terrible indiscretion of his own, and one of the most costly failures of the war. Another clear opportunity at success had clearly been missed, but he ordered an assault nevertheless. At Cold Harbor, seven thousand Union soldiers were killed or wounded, most of them in the first few minutes, while the Confederates lost only fifteen hundred.[255] It was mere butchery.

27 Over the course of all these movements and battles, Robert E. Lee's tactics seemed reactionary, and sometimes desperate, almost always not nearly enough, but after the smoke cleared for the umpteenth time, one could discern his mastery. His strategy was the only one left to him and left to the Confederacy, and it was not hard to figure out, but it was working because he was the one executing it. As the casualties mounted, averaging 2,000 Bluecoats a day for a solid month now,[256] and as Northern hopes were repeatedly dashed, confidence in Ulysses S. Grant waned, and the public outcry against both him and Lincoln— and against the war, itself, started to register at higher and higher decibel levels. Precisely what Grant had hoped to avoid, a stalemate and interminable siege, was the only option Lee afforded him. The two armies were settled, finally, in and around Petersburg, south of Richmond, and the clock was almost sure to run out on the whole war effort.

---

[255] McPherson, *Ordeal by Fire*, p. 423
[256] Catton, *A Stillness at Appomattox*, p. 175

Further south, for Sherman, it was no better. While he did push the army of the South back, Johnston the Lesser now commanding it, he was never offered a full engagement, and Nathan Bedford Forrest hamstrung his every effort.

"I look down towards his feet,"[257] Sherman said of Forrest. Throughout the war, Forrest plagued Sherman and the North. At Fort Donelson, he evaded capture. At Shiloh, a bullet lifted him out of his saddle, but did not kill him—did not even seem to affect him. At Vicksburg, in the early fumbling stages of the campaign, it was Forrest that left Sherman charging all alone the Chickasaw Bluffs. Forrest was here and he was not there, there and not here, and everywhere and nowhere all at once. And then at Fort Pillow, in April 1864, he did what was evil in the sight of the Lord, whether ordering or merely condoning the massacre of surrendering Black troops.[258] "I would follow Forrest to the death, if it cost ten thousand lives and broke the United States' Treasury. For there will be no peace," Sherman realized, "till he is dead."[259]

Indeed, as much mayhem as he caused militarily, what bothered Sherman most was what drove Forrest, and what he let himself stand for: a righteous and tireless hatred, and terroristic zeal, that resisted, boldfaced, the brotherhood of all humanity, and that made every conceivable form of peace unacceptable. "Peace," Forrest once concluded a parley with a Bluecoat officer, "I hate the word, as I hate hell, all niggers, and you."[260]   Such simplicity was infectious, Sherman knew, and

---

[257] Shakespeare, *Othello*, V. ii. 286 (p. 1056)

[258] Judges 2.11, *The New Oxford Annotated Bible*

[259] Sherman, quoted in *Ordeal by Fire*, p. 432

[260] Shakespeare, *Romeo & Juliet*, I. i. 67, 8 (p. 860)

could ripple through both friend and foe, and through all levels of the populace.

"Teach my children to hate," a captain from Virginia told his wife, "with that bitter hate—that bitter and unrelenting hate of the Yankee race that will never permit them to meet under any circumstances without seeking to destroy each other; yea, until Fort Pillow with all its fancied horrors shall appear as insignificant as a schoolboy's tale."[261] And would his wife smile her work to see, that mother of men, when schools themselves would become targets of that bitterness?[262] Would she be satisfied when the People, children and all, begin to kill each other in some sort of meaningless spite, destroying themselves, falling upon one another, stabbing and shooting, biting and eating one another?[263]

And one woman in the North, upon once watching J.E.B. Stuart's marauding Confederates go by, called out after them:

> *"Happy shall they be who pay you back*
> *what you have done to us!*
> *Happy shall they be who take your little ones*
> *and dash them against the rocks!"*[264]

Divinity of Hell![265] It is understandable enough how war can cultivate such feelings, but pride of hatred, however native to

---

[261] McPherson, *For Cause & Comrades*, pp. 149–151

[262] Blake, "The Tyger", *The Norton Anthology of Poetry*, p. 743

[263] Dostoevsky *Crime and Punishment*, p. 547

[264] Psalms 137.8–9, *The New Oxford Annotated Bible*

[265] Shakespeare, *Othello*, II. iii. 333 (p. 1035)

our being, rapacious, insatiable, gives any foreign power leverage over our own souls.

"We are not only fighting hostile armies," Sherman concluded, "but a hostile People."[266] Outside Atlanta, lacking the means to advance forward and take the city, he brooded, and felt more and more precarious by the hour.

28 And with both armies of the North thus bogged down in sieges, factionalism grew strength in Washington and throughout the Union. The People were tired of war. The Democrats, and Copperheads, seeking to gain control, thought they had found their candidate for president: none other than Little Mac, George B. McClellan. He entered the race on an anti-emancipation, peace platform, and by the end of August, 1864, was all but sure to win the election. "So short lived has been the American Union," a foreign observer wrote in an ambiguous tone, "that men who saw it rise will live to see its fall."[267]

Abraham Lincoln went to the People, to citizens, to their representatives, to the army, itself, which constituted an enormous block of eligible voters—a block supposed to throw in with their former commanding general against the President. On September the first, of 1864, the People seemed collectively to say to Abraham Lincoln: "Was it because there were not enough graves in the South that you have taken us there? Is this not the very thing we told you before, 'Let us

---

[266] Sherman, quoted in *Ordeal by Fire*, p. 460
[267] Foote, *The Civil War*, v. 3, p. 85

alone'? For it would have been better for us to have been slaves ourselves than to be dying like this."[268]

But Lincoln begged the People for patience: "Do not be afraid, stand firm, and see the deliverance that the Lord will accomplish.[269] The struggle of today is not altogether for today, don't you see; it is for a vast future also.[270] I, too, want peace. I, too, long for the day when peace will come and come to stay; but it must come so as to be worth the keeping in all future time."[271] Back in the Great Hall, at the podium, he spoke:

"In this great struggle,
  this form of Government
and every form of human right
  is endangered if our enemies succeed.
It is not merely for today,
  but for all time to come
that we should perpetuate
  for our children's children
this great and free government,
  which many, but not nearly all of us
    have enjoyed all our lives.[272]

Fellow citizens,
  we cannot escape history.
No personal significance

[268] Exodus 14.12, *The New Oxford Annotated Bible*
[269] Exodus 14.13, *The New Oxford Annotated Bible*
[270] Lincoln, quoted in *Lincoln's Melancholy*, p. 183
[271] Lincoln, quoted in *Lincoln's Melancholy*, p. 204
[272] Lincoln, quoted in *Lincoln's Melancholy*, p. 205

or insignificance,
can spare one or another of us.

The fiery trial through which we pass,
  will light us down,
    in honor or dishonor,
  to the last generation,
whether we will nobly save,
  or meanly lose,
    the last, best hope on earth."[273]

A strong east wind began to blow on the moment, and it blew all night, every now and again forcing itself into the thoughts of Abraham as he lay restless in his bed.[274] Finally, he rose, quitting the fugue-like state between the acknowledged need for sleep and the world's magnified need for the clarity of his own thoughts, that synaptic space between God's finger and his own, that gap now pregnant with all creation and its chances—or with mere abortion. He went up from his room to another, where he kept maps upon maps on walls and tables, and there the Lord showed him everything—she showed him the whole land: Washington and as far as the Pacific coast, past Virginia and Georgia, past the Mississippi, past the great plains and deserts, past the rocky mountains as far as the Western Sea. "See it with your eyes," the Lord then whispered in his head,[275] and Lincoln closed his eyes and reckoned a thousand acres,[276]

---

[273] Lincoln, quoted in *Lincoln's Melancholy*, p. 190

[274] Exodus 14.21, *The New Oxford Annotated Bible*

[275] Deuteronomy 34.4, *The New Oxford Annotated Bible*

[276] Whitman, *Leaves of Grass* (1855), p. 28

and he comprehended the expanse of the whole earth,[277] and he comprehended the many nations, and the People, all the People, sundry and beautiful and true, and the Lord did seem then to touch his right hand—his calloused writing hand with infinite tenderness.[278] "But you shall not cross over,"[279] she said.

Abraham Lincoln's eyes then opened wide with awe, and then clamped shut in pain of certain knowledge. He spoke as without any breath, "The judgments of the Lord are true and righteous altogether.[280] Naked I came from my mother's womb, and naked shall I return.[281] I believe the cause is to be preferred to men.[282] Blessed," tears streaming now, "be the name of the Lord."[283]

29 The next day, September the second, 1864, William Tecumseh Sherman wired Washington: "I have taken Atlanta." But it was not so much Sherman who took it, as it was Jefferson Davis who gave it to him. Feeling many pressures himself, and maintaining a grudge against Joseph Egglesworth Johnston, Davis shifted course, and replaced his general with another more aggressive one—with another who promised to attack Sherman and to drive him back. And that was precisely the chance Sherman

---

[277] Job 38.18, *The New Oxford Annotated Bible*

[278] Song of Solomon 1:5, *The New Oxford Annotated Bible*

[279] Deuteronomy 34.4, *The New Oxford Annotated Bible*

[280] Lincoln, *The Portable Abraham Lincoln*, p. 321

[281] Job 1.21, *The New Oxford Annotated Bible*

[282] Lincoln, quoted in *Lincoln's Melancholy*, p. 144

[283] Job 1.21, *The New Oxford Annotated Bible*

needed. The Union army parried the attack adeptly, and then pressed and took Atlanta. And Grant then reported a major victory in the Valley of the Shenandoah, cutting off that vital supply source at last from Lee. The end of the war, all of a sudden, drew undeniably near, and on November the eighth, 1864, Abraham Lincoln was reelected president of the United States of America.

Down in Atlanta, so far from his base, Sherman finally decided what he must do. "We cannot change the hearts of these People of the South, but we can make war so terrible, and make them so sick of it that generations will pass away before they would again appeal to it.[284] I will move through Georgia, smashing things to the sea.[285] I will destroy all that they have, and will not spare them, nor man, nor woman, nor child, no, nor infant, and I will slay ox and sheep, horse and donkey.[286] I will make the march, and I will make Georgia howl!"[287]

One of the People of the South, defenseless before the great host of Bluecoats, shouted at the general, "You son of a perverse, rebellious woman!"[288]

"War is cruelty, Madame" Sherman deigned to reply, "and you cannot refine it.[289] You have not rejected President

---

[284] Sherman, quoted in *Ordeal by Fire*, p. 460

[285] Sherman, quoted in *Ordeal by Fire*, p. 460

[286] 1 Samuel 15.3, *The New Oxford Annotated Bible*

[287] Sherman, quoted in *Ordeal by Fire*, p. 460

[288] 1 Samuel 20.30, *The New Oxford Annotated Bible*

[289] Sheman, quoted in *Ordeal by Fire*, p. 159

Lincoln, but the Lord; and you will cry out because of your king, whom you have chosen for yourselves."[290]

A grim eternity of war and the hardening of many hearts had gone into his orders, and into the execution of them, romance of war and knightly chivalry dissolved forever in the terrible acid of enmity and hatred, settlement by the sword coming at last to mean all-out war, modern style, with a blow at the economic potential cutting across the farmer's yard and dooming people innocent enough to the loss of a lifetime's hard-bought gains.[291]

But Abraham Lincoln spoke to the People of the South and of the North, and to all the People of every time and place on the earth in a different way:

> *"Four years ago, both parties deprecated war;*
>> *but one of them would make war*
>>> *rather than let the nation survive;*
>> *and the other would accept war*
>>> *rather than let it perish.*
> *Neither party expected for the war,*
>> *the magnitude, or the duration,*
>>> *which it has already attained.*
> *Neither anticipated that the cause of the conflict*
>> *might cease with, or even before,*
>>> *the conflict itself should cease.*
> *Each looked for an easier triumph,*
>> *and a result less fundamental and astounding.*

---

[290] 1 Samuel 8.18, *The New Oxford Annotated Bible*
[291] Catton, *A Stillness at Appomattox*, p. 276

If we shall suppose that Slavery
is one of those offenses which,
having continued through the Lord's appointed time,
she now wills to remove,
and that she gives both North and South,
this terrible war,
as the woe due to those by whom the offence came,
shall we discern therein
any departure from those divine attributes
which the believers in a Living God
always ascribe to her?

Fondly do we hope—fervently do we pray—
that the mighty scourge of war
may speedily pass away."

It was his second inaugural address, and he drew a long breath.

"Yet, if God wills that it continue,
until all the wealth piled by the bond-man's
two hundred and fifty years of unrequited toil
shall be sunk,
and until every drop of blood drawn with the lash,
shall be paid by another drawn with the sword,
as was said three thousand years ago,
so still it must be said,
'The judgments of the Lord are true and righteous altogether.'

The assembled crowd listened in sober recognition of both his resolution and its sacrifice. And then he intoned:

"With malice toward none;
with charity for all;
with firmness in the right,
as God gives us to see the right,
let us strive on to finish the work we are in;
to bind up the nation's wounds;
to care for him who shall have borne the battle,
and for his widow, and his orphan—
to do all which may achieve and cherish a just,
and a lasting peace,
among ourselves,
and with all nations."[292]

He spoke under the finally completed dome of the Capitol Building, atop of which stood a statue; and there upon that statue, a few of the People noted, a dove did light.

---

[292] Lincoln, *The Portable Abraham Lincoln*, pp. 320, 1

VI

 Just before Christmas, 1864, William Tecumseh Sherman's army of the North took Savannah, the city near the sea, and the endpoint of his destructive march.

And before February, the United States Congress passed the thirteenth amendment, abolishing slavery forever. "There is power in words," the President said on the occasion,

"and there is power in conviction.
Beneath all the differences of race and religion,
faith and station,
we are one People.
But, of course, true unity cannot be so easily won.
It starts with a change in attitudes—
a broadening of our minds,
and a broadening of our hearts.[293]

The perspective of the People is not perfect,
but by the startling foresight of our founders—
by the glorious allowance,
and definitional injunction of our Constitution,
of our code and our creed,
of our very natures,
we may and we must strive always
to see and perform truer justice,
so as never to condemn our progeny
to the dogmas of our folly.

---

[293] Obama, *Barack Obama*, p. 24 and Blurb

With all my heart,
   I celebrate the passage of the thirteenth amendment,
      which does not seek to alter the will of the Lord,
      but only to recognize and further realize it.

So may we all,
   the whole world over,
      each in our own way,
   come to celebrate also this event
      as immortal and sublime,[294]
         blessed be the name of the Lord."[295]

In early April, Ulysses S. Grant did finally dislodge Robert E. Lee and the proud Army of Northern Virginia from Petersburg, and the army of the North was marching again, this time in hot pursuit of the fleeing confederates. It was a bad road to march on, like all the roads of war—deeply rutted, fouled by the march of the cavalry up ahead, by turns heavy with mud and deep with the dust that would make marching a gray choking agony. But it was the road the army had been marching toward from the very beginning, and many thousands of soldiers had died in order that this road might at last be marched on; for this was the road to the end of the war, and on over the horizon to the unimaginable beginnings and endings that would lie beyond that. Also, and more intimately, for both armies indeed, it was the beginning of the long road home.[296]

---

[294] McPherson, *Ordeal by Fire*, p. 467
[295] Job 1.21, *The New Oxford Annotated Bible*
[296] Catton, *A Stillness at Appomattox*, pg. 373

And Union soldiers did enter both Petersburg and Richmond. Jefferson Davis had fled some days before, and was now in hiding. The Confederates eventually launched a hopeless counterattack, and for the last time, the army of the North heard the high, spine-tingling wail of the Rebel yell, a last great shout of defiance, a yell even as Stonewall had ordered so long ago at First Manassas.[297] The attack broke like a wave upon the shore, with much sound and fury, but signified nothing.[298]

At Appomattox Courthouse the following day, Robert E. Lee surrendered his army. He said to Grant, "I went away full, but the Lord has brought me back empty; why call me Robert E. Lee of the South, when the Lord has dealt so harshly with me?"[299] He lifted his eyes to his adversary, and said, "Now you may call me Robert E. Lee, your prisoner, and prisoner of the North."

But Ulysses looked squarely at the great general, favored of heaven so highly, the man who fought so long and valiantly, and who had suffered so much more than he could know,[300] and then said, "I will call you Robert E. Lee of the United States of America, of the North and the South, and of the Lord, our God, and of all her People."

The Lord delighted in these words, and then turned to Jefferson Davis where he was hiding, and said, "Have you considered Abraham Lincoln? There is no one like him on

[297] Catton, *A Stillness at Appomattox*, pg. 376, 7

[298] Shakespeare, *Macbeth*, V. v. 27, 8 (p. 1133)

[299] Ruth 1.21, *The New Oxford Annotated Bible*

[300] Grant, *The Personal Memoirs*, p. 721

earth.[301]   And yet every atom belonging to him as good belongs to you."[302]

Jefferson Davis said defiantly, "It is better for me to die than to live."[303]

The Lord asked, "Have you learned lessons only of those who admired you, and were tender with you, and stood aside for you? Have you not learned great lessons from those who reject you, and brace themselves against you? Or who treat you with contempt, or dispute the passage of you?"[304]

Jefferson Davis replied, with his one good eye glaring in the face of the Lord, "O, I am angry!"

"Will you condemn me," the Lord then asked, "that you may be justified?[305] Is it right for you to be angry?"[306]

"Yes," Jefferson responded quickly, "and I am angry enough to die."

The Lord could see that his heart was hardened,[307] and so she did not speak to him again.

[301] Job 1.8, *The New Oxford Annotated Bible*
[302] Whitman, *Leaves of Grass* (1855), p. 27
[303] Jonah 4.3, *The New Oxford Annotated Bible*
[304] Whitman, "Stronger Lessons", p. 631
[305] Job 40.8, *The New Oxford Annotated Bible*
[306] Jonah 4.4, *The New Oxford Annotated Bible*
[307] Exodus 14.8, *The New Oxford Annotated Bible*

The war ended, and in the North, Frederick Douglass, the Runaway, tireless, and brave, started to sing:

> *"O, I will sing to the Lord*
> > *for she has triumphed gloriously.*
> *The Lord is my strength and my might,*
> > *and she has become my salvation.*[308]

O, People, my People, People of the United States,
> *let freedom ring.*
Let freedom ring
> *from the prodigious hilltops of New Hampshire.*
Let freedom ring
> *from the mighty mountains of New York.*
Let freedom ring
> *from the heightening Alleghenies of Pennsylvania.*
Let freedom ring
> *from the snowcapped Rockies of Colorado.*
Let freedom ring
> *from the curvaceous slopes of California.*

> *But not only that.*
Let freedom ring
> *from Stone Mountain of Georgia.*
Let freedom ring
> *from Lookout Mountain in Tennessee.*
Let freedom ring
> *from every hill and molehill of Mississippi.*
From every mountain side, let freedom ring.

---

[308] Exodus 15.1, and 15.2, *The New Oxford Annotated Bible*

When we all let freedom ring—
when we let it ring
from every village and every hamlet,
from every state and every city,
we will be able to speed up that day
when all of God's children,
black men and white men,
Jews and Gentiles,
Protestants and Catholics—
all the People all over the earth
will be able to join hands and sing
in the words of the old Negro spiritual,
"Free at last, Free at last,
Thank God all mighty, we are free at last."[309]

In the morning of April 14, 1865, Abraham Lincoln's wife Mary Todd looked upon her husband and said, "God has brought laughter for me, and everyone who hears will laugh with me."[310]   And Abraham did laugh with her, heartily, and they embraced as they had never embraced before.

And then Abraham said, "The Lord is our God, the Lord alone, and we shall love her, and love her People with all our heart, and with all our soul, and with all our might. You and I, Mary, and all must keep these words in our hearts always. We all must recite them to our children and talk about them when we are at home and when we are away, when we lie down and when we rise.[311]   This nation of nations must develop an

---

[309] Martin Luther King Jr., "I Have a Dream" (1963)
[310] Genesis 21.6, *The New Oxford Annotated Bible*
[311] Deuteronomy 6.4-7, *The New Oxford Annotated Bible*

overriding loyalty to mankind as a whole.[312] Our loyalties must become ecumenical rather than sectional.[313] Every kind of man and woman and child, the 'poor white' in the South, the North, and in the west, the same as the Black, and the immigrant just off the boat, or over the border—all whom tyranny has oppressed, all who need help, deserves the best we can be. All my experiences in the hospitals, among the soldiers in the crowd of the cities, with the masses, in the great centers of population—allowing for all idiosyncrasies, idiocrasies, passions, what not, the very worst—have only served to confirm my faith in People—in the average of People, all of one instinct, one race, one whole, addicted to the same vices, ennobled by the same virtues: dignity, courtesy, open-handedness, radical in all, beautiful in all![314] O, Mary, Mary, die when I may, I want it said of me by those who know me best, by you, my dear wife, that I always plucked a thistle and planted a flower where I thought a flower would grow."[315]

"Talk you of death?"[316] Mary Todd responded, "Wherefore should we speak of death now?" And she smiled. Then she laughed. And her husband laughed with her again, and they held one another.

And then on April 14, 1865, it was Good Friday, in the evening at Ford's Theater, Abraham Lincoln, the sixteenth president of these United States of America, watching a

---

[312] Martin Luther King, Jr., from "Beyond Vietnam" (1967)

[313] Martin Luther King, Jr., "Christmas Sermon on Peace" (1967)

[314] Whitman, quoted in *Walt Whitman Speaks*, pp. 121, 2

[315] Lincoln, quoted in *Lincoln's Melancholy*, p. 203

[316] Shakespeare, *Othello*, V. ii. 38

comedy called *Our American Cousin* with his wife Mary Todd, was shot in the head and murdered.

32 Abraham was buried five days later. General Ulysses S. Grant wept openly at the funeral service, and millions stood silently along the tracks as a nine-car train carried Lincoln's body back to Springfield, Illinois.[317] Walt Whitman, the old gray poet, dwelling among the People[318], and commensurate with the People[319], cried in anguish, looking up at the finished dome atop the Capitol Building:

> *"The ship is anchored safe and sound,*
> *its voyage closed and done,*
> *From fearful trip the victor ship comes in with object won;*
> *Exult O shores, and ring O bells!*
> *But I with mournful tread,*
> *Walk the deck my captain lies,*
> *Fallen cold and dead."[320]*

And Jefferson Davis rose too, when he heard the news— rose in disbelief, from where he was ensconced; and coming to a window, he said:

> *"I had uttered what I did not understand,*
> *I had heard the Lord by the hearing of the ear,*

---

[317] McPherson, *Ordeal by Fire*, p. 483

[318] Exodus 29.46, *The New Oxford Annotated Bible*

[319] Whitman, *Leaves of Grass* (1855), p. 7

[320] Whitman, "O Captain! My Captain!", pp. 467–468

but now my eye sees you;
therefore I despise myself,
and repent in dust and ashes."[321]

Tears then fell from both his eyes, even as they did when a little more than one year earlier, his son Joseph fell from the balcony of the executive mansion in Richmond and died of a fractured skull.[322] Sobbing now filled his little room, but when the luxury of tears, and pain within his breast and bones had passed away,[323]—an eternity later, he was angry no longer, and he opened the window, and called out,

"Sing, O Lord, sing for ever and ever,
sing to the better angels of our nature,
sing, Lord, O sing!"

33

And the Lord, the God of the United States of America, sings:

"I mourn, and yet shall mourn
with ever-returning spring.
Ever returning spring, to me you will bring[324]
the thought of him I love,
one of the greatest, sweetest souls everyway,
nowhere a more conclusive argument
in favor of People as they average up.[325]
Abraham! of the west, and east,
of the North, and South,

---

[321] Job 42.5-6, *The New Oxford Annotated Bible*

[322] McPherson, *Ordeal by Fire*, p. 484

[323] Homer, *The Iliad*, p. 584

[324] Whitman, "When Lilacs Last…", p. 459

[325] Whitman, quoted in *Walt Whitman Speaks*, p. 133

of the People—of all the People of all the world,
a hero august and simple as nature—
supreme for his own ends,
his own eligibility,[326]
an American...

Praised be the fathomless universe,
For life and joy, and for objects and knowledge curious,
And for love, sweet love—every type of love,
praise! praise! praise![327]
Every thing without exception has an eternal soul!
The trees have, rooted in the ground!
the weeds of the sea have!
and animals![328]
O secret of the earth and sky!...[329]

Lo, body and soul—this land,
with spires, and the sparkling and hurrying tides,
and the ships,
The varied and ample land,
the South and the North in the light.
Pictures of growing spring and farms and homes,
With the Fourth-month eve at sundown,
and the gray smoke lucid and bright,
With floods of the yellow gold of the gorgeous,
indolent, sinking sun,
burning, expanding the air,
With the fresh sweet herbage under foot,

[326] Whitman, quoted in *Walt Whitman Speaks*, p. 133
[327] Whitman, "When Lilacs Last...", p. 464
[328] Whitman, "To Think of Time", p. 557
[329] Whitman, "Passage to India", p. 539

and the pale green leaves of the trees prolific,
In the distance the flowing glaze, the breast of the river,
    with a wind-dapple here and there,
With ranging hills on the banks,
    with many a line against the sky, and shadows,
And ever the far-spreading prairies
    covered with grass and corn,
And the city at hand with dwellings so dense,
    and stacks of chimneys,
And all the scenes of life and the workshops,
    and the workmen and women
        homeward returning.[330]

I saw askant the armies,
I saw as in noiseless dreams hundreds of battle flags,
Borne through the smoke of the battle
    and pierced with missiles I saw them,
And carried hither and yon through the smoke,
    and torn and bloody,
And at last but a few shreds left on the staffs,
And the staffs all splintered and broken.

I saw the battle-corpses, myriads of them,
And the white skeletons of the young, and old,
    of man, of woman, and child,
And I saw the debris and debris
    of all the slain People of the war.[331]

It is not to diffuse you that you were born
    of your mother and father,

---

[330] Whitman, "When Lilacs Last...", pp. 462-3
[331] Whitman, "When Lilacs Last...", p. 466

it is to identify you,
It is not that you should be undecided,
but that you should be decided,
Something long preparing and formless
is arrived and formed in you,
You are henceforth secure, whatever comes or goes.[332]

The Americans of all nations at any time upon the earth
have the fullest poetical nature.
The United States themselves
are essentially the greatest poem.[333]

I see male and female everywhere,
I see the serene brotherhood of philosophs,
I see ranks, colors, barbarisms, civilizations,
and I go among them,
I mix indiscriminately,
I salute all the inhabitants of the earth.
Health to you!
good will to you all,
from me and from America sent!
Each of us inevitable,
Each of us limitless—
Each of us with his or her right upon the earth,
Each of us allowed the eternal purports of the earth,
Each of us here as divinely as any is here.[334]

I sing my song and rain tears on the earth in the Spring,
earth and sky and sea twined

---

[332] Whitman, "Who Learns My Lesson Complete?", p. 517

[333] Whitman, *Leaves of Grass* (1855), p. 5

[334] Whitman "Salut Au Monde!" pp. 294-5

with the chant of my own soul,
here in the fragrant pines and the cedars dusk and dim:[335]
I sing for him whom I love, and for all his own,
I sing for you, whoever you are!
And for you of centuries hence when you listen to me!
And for you each and everywhere whom I specify not,
but include just the same![336]

No, the earth is not an echo,
and this man and his life and all things of his life
are well-considered.[337]

Remember Abraham, O People, my People,
remember him and his,
remember yourselves,
always."

---

[335] Whitman, "When Lilacs Last…", p. 467
[336] Whitman "Salut Au Monde!" pp. 294–5
[337] Whitman, "To Think of Time", p. 554

Acknowledgements

Lincoln's Melancholy, by Joshua Wolf Shenk, if not my primary resource here, was certainly my inspiration for this new effort. It did for this project what Whitman claims Emerson did for him: "brought me to a boil." Shenk's work is totally different from my own, but, aside from providing a compelling and inspiring portrait of Abraham Lincoln, it, more importantly, reminded me of the responsibility that has always been, for me, so much a part of the impulse of study. All of a sudden, that old college paper had a solid, driving heartbeat, and only I could attest to it. And because of Shenk's example, I had to.

In the least, I hope my effort encourages others to read Shenk's wonderful book, or any of the many other works I have tapped into here, *The Bible* most especially, Whitman's *Leaves*, everything and anything touched by Shakespeare, and, of course, the actual words of those who both navigated and directed the war, themselves. Without exception, every book I use here is magnificent, and if I could escort you to it or to another, to Foote, Catton, McPherson, or Kendi, and to the help it provides me presently, I would feel very much fulfilled in this endeavor.

Whatever I have achieved, I am perfectly aware it could not have been done without the love and support of my family and friends. Thanks, especially, to my mother and father for their help, and inspiration. To Chad Gordon, this would all still be a bunch of notes in a box in my basement if not for your example and help. Thank you. To Suzy, your belief in me is the call I strive to answer in everything. Thank you for your encouragement and patience. And, of course, to my favorite teacher (—to everyone's favorite teacher) Professor David Hadas, every word of this project is a tribute to you. Thanks for encouraging me to write my own kinds of papers.

Note to My Professor

(in *Bible as Literature*, at Washington University in St. Louis, 1994):

Initially I intended to write a paper on the limitless power of interpretation, on "the omnipotence of theologians." I hoped to show the power of God in every person—the power which she uses whenever she reads a book, whenever he selects a quotation, whenever she provides a schism of faith with each breath she breathes out into space, whether he knows it or not. Indeed, I also wished to show the power of God in post-*Bible* creators—writers and leaders, whose works are no less deserving of worship than any other.

But I decided against that paper. Why should I merely state a belief and not test it? Therefore, I gave my theory a try: I wrote a biblical history of the American Civil War, appropriating a new god, creating a new "spiritual" context. I used several quotations (not all of them from the *Bible*) in the context of my own choosing, which posed some problems, but nothing a "theologian" couldn't handle.

And that is not all I did, you will see.

Bibliography

Angelou, Maya. *All God's Children Need Traveling Shoes.* Knopf Doubleday Publishing Group, 1986.

Bakewell, Sarah. At the Existentialist Cafe: Freedom, Being, and Apricot Cocktails. Great Britain, Chatto & Windus, 2016.

Catton, Bruce. *A Stillness at Appomattox.* First Anchor Books Edition, 1990.

Delbanco, Andrew. *The Portable Abraham Lincoln.* New York: Viking Penguin, a division of Penguin Group USA, Inc., 1992.

Dostoevsky, Fyodor. *Crime and Punishment,* translated by Richard Pevear and Larissa Volokhonsky. New York: Vintage Books, a division of Random House, Inc., 1992.

Ferguson, Margaret, Salter, Mary Jo, and Stallworthy, Jon. *The Norton Anthology of Poetry, Fifth Edition.* W. W. Norton & Company, Inc., 2005.

Foote, Shelby. The Civil War: A Narrative: v. 1. Fort Sumter to Perryville--v. 2. Fredericksburg to Meridian--v. 3. Red River to Appomattox. New York: First Vintage Books Edition, 1986.

Frost, Robert. *Robert Frost: Collected Poems, Prose, & Plays.* Literary Classics of the United States, Inc. New York: Penguin Putnam Inc., 1995.

Hafiz. *The Gift: Poems by Hafiz The Great Sufi Master,* translated by Daniel Ladinsky. Penguin Publishing Group, 1999.

Harbage, Alfred. *William Shakespeare: The Complete Works.* New York: Penguin Books, Inc., 1969.

Homer. *The Iliad,* translated by Robert Fitzgerald. Alfred A. Knopf, Inc. 1974.

Homer. *The Odyssey,* translated by Robert Fitzgerald. New York: Farrar, Straus and Giroux, Inc., 1998.

Kelly-Gangi, Carol. *Barack Obama: His Essential Wisdom.* New York: Fall River Press, 2016.

Kendi, Ibram X. *Stamped from the Beginning: The Definitive History of Racist Ideas in America.* New York: Hachette Book Group, Inc. 2016.

Marszalek, John F. *The Personal Memoirs of Ulysses S. Grant.* Cambridge, Massachusetts: The Belknap Press of Harvard University Press, 2017.

McPherson, James M. For *Cause & Country: Why Men Fought in the Civil War.* New York: Oxford University Press, Inc., 1997.

McPherson, James M. The Negro's Civil War: How American Blacks Felt and Acted During the War for the Union. New York: Anchor Books, a division of Random House, Inc., 2003.

McPherson, James M. *Ordeal by Fire: Volume II, The Civil War*. McGraw-Hill, Inc., 1993.

Metzger, Bruce M. and Murphy, Roland E. *The New Oxford Annotated Bible*. Oxford University Press, Inc., 1994.

Nevin, David. *The Road to Shiloh: Early Battles in the West: The Civil War*. Time-Life Books Inc., 1985.

Rumi. *The Essential Rumi*, translated by Coleman Barks. HarperCollins Publishers, 2004.

Shenk, Joshua Wolf. Lincoln's Melancholy: How Depression Challenged a President and Fueled His Greatness. New York: Houghton Mifflin Harcourt Publishing Company, 2005.

Sophocles. *The Oedipus Cycle: Oedipus Rex, Oedipus at Colonus, Antigone*, translated by Dudley Fitts and Robert Fitzgerald. Orlando, Florida: Harcourt, Inc., 1949.

Virgil. *The Aeneid*, translated by Robert Fitzgerald. New York: Vintage Books, a division of Random House, Inc., 1990.

Wineapple, Brenda. *Walt Whitman Speaks*. New York, N.Y.: Literary Classics of the United States, Inc., 2019.

Whicher, Stephen E. *Selections from Ralph Waldo Emerson: An Organic Anthology*. Boston: Houghton Mifflin Company, 1957.

Whitman, Walt. *Whitman: Poetry and Prose*. Literary Classics of the United States, Inc. New York: Penguin Random House Inc., 1982.

CPSIA information can be obtained
at www.ICGtesting.com
Printed in the USA
LVHW090229100820
662779LV00005B/53/J

9 781087 898285